DEMON SWORN

THE WITCH'S REBELS BOOK THREE

Demon Sworn
Copyright © 2018 by Sarah Piper
SarahPiperBooks.com

ISBN-13: 978-1-948455-08-4

ALSO BY SARAH PIPER

THE WITCH'S REBELS

Shadow Kissed

Darkness Bound

Demon Sworn

Blood Cursed

Death Untold

Rebel Reborn

THE WITCH'S MONSTERS

Blood and Midnight

VAMPIRE ROYALS OF NEW YORK

Dorian & Charlotte

Dark Deception

Dark Seduction

Dark Obsession

Gabriel & Jacinda

Heart of Thorns

Heart of Fury

Heart of Flames

TAROT ACADEMY

ONE

ASHER

Fucking hell. What have you done to me, Cupcake?

I could still taste her on my lips. Still feel the silk of her hair between my fingers. Still smell the raw, earthy scent of her desire as she lost control at my touch.

My cock stiffened at the *very* recent memory; my heart was still hammering from the state she'd left me in.

But when I stared down at the ground outside my cell where she should've been lying, there was only cold, damp rock.

She'd attacked Jonathan. Sucked out his rotten soul. I kept waiting to see the iridescent bubble of her magical shield, but it never materialized.

In the blink of an eye, they'd both just… vanished.

If it wasn't for his blood staining the ground, I might've thought I'd imagined the whole damn thing.

Had Gray known it'd go down like that? I knew she felt responsible for Jonathan, that she had to deal with him on her own terms. But where the fuck had she taken him? What was her end game?

"A little warning would've been nice, Cupcake."

Shaking off the last of my shock, I pushed myself out of the chair and got to my feet. The room tipped, then righted, but this time it wasn't because of the damn devil's trap nano-whatevers that psycho hunter had injected me with. Gray's power had neutralized them, replenishing my own power in spades. Raw energy coursed through me. I felt stronger and more alive than I'd felt in ages, all of my senses magnified.

My blood was absolutely humming with her magic.

It felt... fucking *amazing*.

As soon as you're back, Cupcake, I'm going to return the favor... times a thousand.

I was just trying to figure out my game plan for finding the other witches in this dank-ass prison when I picked up on sounds in the corridor—heavy footsteps and conversation.

"...stringing along the little piss-ant for another week," one guy was saying. "Two, tops."

"You're assuming he doesn't have any more tricks up his sleeve," another dude replied. "Far as I'm concerned, the sooner the old man takes control, the better."

The footsteps stopped, and I heard the click of a lighter, followed by the unmistakable crackle of a cigarette being sucked to life.

In a rough voice, dude number one said, "Kid's a fuck-up, Shears. Always has been. Smoke?"

"Fuck no. That shit'll kill you faster than vamp blood."

"Suit yourself." Smokey Joe took another drag, then said, "Don't hold your breath waiting on the old man. He talks a good game, but he won't make a move as long as Jonathan's alive. Can't risk the kid fucking things up with Orendiel."

Orendiel? The only asshole I'd ever heard of with a dickhead name like that was a fae soldier I'd met about fifty years back. From what I remembered, he was trying to work his way up the ranks in one of the dark courts, but he'd accidentally killed some prick royal heir and started a war instead.

Seemed to me those fuckers were always fighting, anyway.

Could it be the same guy was now working with *this* shitshow?

"You seen him lately?" Shears asked. "Kid's going downhill fast."

"So?" Smokey Joe laughed. "Last time I checked, he was still breathing."

"We'll see." Shears waited a beat, then said, "Where is that little fuckstain, anyway?"

"Should be down in B-block. He went to deal with the witch and her demon pet."

"Are you fucking kidding me? That was an hour ago!" Shears groaned. "Come on, we'd better check it out. Sounds like he needs some adult supervision."

Smokey Joe laughed. "Maybe the witch needs some adult supervision. Preferably in the form of a spanking."

Shears laughed.

"Think she likes it rough?" Smokey's footsteps started up again, and I tried to hold myself back from leaping out of the cell and beating both their asses.

"You can't fuck a witch," Shears said, jogging to catch up. "She'll turn your dick into a toad. You'll croak every time you come."

They both cracked up at that.

"As long as I'm inside that tight little ass," Smokey Joe said, "I don't give a fuck *what* it sounds like when I come."

The power humming through my blood turned to rage, heating me from the inside, making me shake all over again.

Laugh it up, motherfuckers. I'm going to kill you in the bloodiest way possible.

They were getting close. A quick scan of the cell I'd been trapped in revealed nothing useful—Jonathan had been careful not to leave any weapons or sharp tools around. I could take a chance and try to hit one of them with the chair, but that would leave me too exposed to the other guy, especially if they were packing weapons.

With no easy escape route, I dropped back into the chair and slumped forward. They were expecting a weak, impotent demon held captive by a devil's trap injected right into my bloodstream.

So that's what they were gonna get.

For a minute, anyway.

Smokey Joe arrived first. Dude was built like a tank, complete with a square head set off by a square buzz cut. A brutal scar curled around his neck, and his biceps were covered in tribal tattoos I was pretty sure he didn't know the meaning of.

His inner forearm was branded with some kind of symbol. Celtic, maybe?

He took one look at the open gate and me slumped in the chair, and said, "Why the fuck is this open?"

I said nothing.

"Speak, hellspawn," he barked.

I lifted my head, barely meeting his eyes. "Jon... Jonathan," I panted. "Tormenting me."

Shears appeared behind Smokey. He was about my size, with the same tattoos and Celtic brand as his partner. Both men were human, mid-forties, dressed in nondescript black T-shirts, camouflage pants, and boots.

Their pockets bulged, but I was pretty sure it wasn't because they were happy to see me. They were packing, geared up like some kind of cave militia.

"Why the fuck would Jonathan give you a chance to escape?" Shears asked.

"Can't escape," I said, lowering my voice as though it was costing me a lot of energy to speak. "Can't move. He... torments."

Smokey Joe laughed, his lungs wheezing. "Gotta hand it to the little fucker. He makes torture an art form."

The men entered the cell, daring to step closer.

"So where is he?" Shears asked me.

"Fuck Jonathan." Smokey Joe grabbed his cock and laughed. "I wanna know where that little cunt witch is at."

"Fuck… you," I panted. Even a weak, impotent demon like me couldn't let him get away with that kind of talk.

Shears grinned, pulling a baton from a metal loop on the back of his belt. It looked like a police baton, but it was carved in runes and symbols.

Another devil's trap.

"I say we smoke him," Shears said, touching the baton to my shoulder. I flinched for show, but I didn't feel a damn thing.

Gray's magic seemed to have immunized me from those symbols.

How is this even possible?

"Ease off, Shears." Smokey fished a pack of Camels from one of his many pockets and shook out a smoke. He cupped his hands around the lighter to light it, even though there wasn't any wind in here, and sucked in a deep drag. "Where is he, demon?"

Smoke clouded my eyes. I forced out a cough. "I said, fuck—"

He cracked my jaw with a right hook, damn near dislocating it. I heard the bone pop, but barely felt the pain. The bone was already sliding back into place.

It hadn't even had time to swell up.

That was the power of Gray's magic.

Thank you, Cupcake.

"Top… topside," I moaned, slurring my speech a little. "Something about more… more witches."

"*What* witches?" Shears asked. "Where?"

I didn't respond. I needed them riled up and distracted.

The more rage that blinded them, the sloppier they'd become.

Right on cue, Shears kicked the chair out from under me, sending me sprawling on the floor.

He was definitely the bad cop in their operation.

I moaned and groaned, then braced for the kick in the ribs I knew would come next.

The force of it cracked my sternum.

Damn, these assholes are predictable.

"Please," I begged. "I'll tell you whatever... Just... make it stop." I gasped for air, but my ribs were already healed.

Short of beheading, it seemed there wasn't much they could do to hurt me.

Smokey knelt down in front of me, blowing a plume of smoke in my face. "Tell us everything you know."

"He... he was talking to Gray about a... a coven. In town somewhere."

"And the witch?" Smokey asked.

"Took her as... bait. A way in with the other witches. Surprise attack."

"What else?"

I pressed my advantage, recalling their earlier conversation about "the old man" who was supposed to take over for Jonathan. "Something about... finding his own way. Secret experiments. Didn't want the old man to know."

"Shit." Smokey Joe glanced up at Shears, and I knew I'd hit the mark. "Get Duke on the line."

Shears removed a device from another pocket—some kind of souped-up cell phone—and made the call.

"The kid is AWOL," he said to Duke. "Topside, we think. Some kind of coven. Yeah, send someone to investigate."

He glanced at Smokey while Duke responded, then said, "What do you want them to do when they find him?"

Smokey didn't hesitate. "End it."

"You heard the man," Shears said, then disconnected the call. Kicking me again for old time's sake, he said, "So, we smoking this motherfucker or what?"

Smokey Joe got to his feet and shook his head. "The old man wants all prisoners kept alive."

Shears shrugged. "Fair enough."

He wound up once again, and I prepared to make out with the business end of his boot.

The douchebag didn't disappoint.

Smokey Joe flicked his spent butt at my face. "Thank you for your cooperation, hellspawn. I'm sure we'll be seeing each other again real soon."

Count on it, dickless.

I waited until the two of them turned their backs.

Then I leaped to my feet and charged.

I took Smokey Joe first, grabbing his head and twisting it around until his neck snapped. He dropped like a sack of bricks, and then I was on Shears.

He was no match for my strength. I wrestled him down and bashed his head against the ground.

"And for the record," I said, "those are some *bullshit* tattoos."

After a brief recon down the corridor to make sure no

one else was in the vicinity, I returned to the cell and searched the guards, removing the devil's trap baton, Smokey's lighter, a pair of high-tech stun guns, four knives, a flashlight, and a fat wallet full of what looked like black credit cards without numbers or names.

I also took the comms devices—souped-up phones, just as I'd suspected. They worked underground, and also contained GPS trackers and maps of the entire cave system.

Since Shears and I were similar in size, I stripped off his clothes and quickly changed into them, especially grateful for the steel-toed boots.

Yeah, the ol' switcheroo was probably the oldest trick in the book, but there was a reason it was such a classic move: It usually worked.

Plus, I looked damn good in camo.

Locked and loaded with my new gear, I grinned at the men slumped at my feet. "Thank you for *your* cooperation, assholes."

Then I lit the bodies on fire and headed out in search of the witches of Blackmoon Bay.

TWO

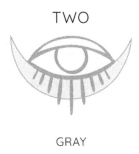

GRAY

Fire, ash, and blood.

It was all I could see, all I could smell, and—no matter how hard I tried to spit it out—all I could taste. My throat burned as I panted and gasped my way across a barren, rocky terrain in search of water. I couldn't remember the last time I'd had any.

How long had I been wandering this forsaken place? Days? Weeks?

I was exhausted, my body little more than a collection of bruises and bloody gashes that throbbed painfully with every beat of my heart. I had no shoes. It hurt to walk. To breathe. To exist. And the magic I'd worked so hard to unlock with my book of shadows ritual had all but fizzled out. Tapping into it now felt like trying to start a campfire in the rain. A spark, then a fizzle. A puff of smoke that quickly disappeared.

The possibility that my magic was permanently spent

was frightening enough. But if I didn't find water soon, I was pretty sure I wouldn't have to worry about magic—or anything else, for that matter.

Where the hell am I?

I reached the top of a jagged black ridge and sat down to catch my breath, scanning the horizon. Acrid smoke roiled in the distance. With every painful breath, it singed my lungs and brought tears to my eyes. The wind kicked up, and a storm of ash swirled around me like snow, falling endlessly from a sky so black I wondered if I'd been swallowed by some great, terrible beast.

I pulled my shirt up over my mouth and waited for the wind to die down again.

One thing I'd learned about this place: the fires were a constant.

So was the thirst.

I closed my eyes and rubbed my temples, trying to chase down a memory—a clue—but nothing came. The last thing I remembered clearly was being at the safe house. Falling asleep on the couch, curled up in Asher's arms…

Asher…

I gasped as a sliver of memory peeked through the fog. It was no more than a flash—a whisper of warm breath ghosting across my neck, rough hands running up my back, a kiss that tasted like cinnamon—and then it was gone.

Damn. The memories were so close to the surface, but the harder I chased them, the faster they ran.

I opened my eyes again and tried to orient myself.

Where was I, exactly? How had I gotten here? Had

someone taken me? Where were the guys? Were they out wandering over these inhospitable black rocks, looking for me like I'd been looking for them?

And why was the front of my shirt covered in someone else's blood?

I scraped my tongue along my upper teeth, trying in vain to get rid of that sharp, coppery taste.

No luck.

It didn't add up. Witches weren't vampires—none of us had ever survived the change. The thought of drinking blood curdled my stomach. How the hell had it gotten in my mouth? On my clothes?

More importantly—who did it belong to? I was pretty sure it wasn't mine.

Had I... had I *killed* someone? Another vampire? A human?

Water, Gray. Water. Maybe something edible. Those are your priorities.

Hitting the pause button on my morbid thoughts, I grabbed a sharp rock and used it to tear off the bottoms of my pant legs, then tied the fabric around my bare feet. The rocks were only getting sharper, and I had no idea how much longer I'd have to walk. As far as I knew, I hadn't seen any signs of life—water, birds, even centipedes or fire ants would've been a welcome sight.

But no matter how high I scrambled up the ridge, all I could see were more jagged peaks, rising up through the smoke. The vista was endless; from up on the ridge, it looked like a vast sea of torn tissue paper layered in shades of gray and black.

Aside from the fact that it was trying to kill me, the place was actually kind of beautiful.

I continued on, one painstakingly slow step at a time. But my makeshift shoe came undone and caught on a rock, sending me tumbling. I hit the ground with a grunt, slicing both my palms.

Great. More blood.

I got to my knees and inspected the wounds, watching as my blood dripped onto the rocks below.

Then it began to glow. Faintly at first, then stronger, pulsing like a bright beacon.

It was the first sign of my magic since I'd started wandering this place, and I leaped on it ferociously, slamming my palms against the earth, ignoring the stinging bite of the rocks.

Power surged up my arms and across my back, igniting my senses and kicking them into overdrive. I could smell the fires up close now, like sulfur and coal. The bloody taste in my mouth sharpened. All around me, I could hear the ash falling softly to the ground. And deep inside me, my magic was stirring back to life, warming my chest and vibrating out through my fingers and toes.

Something shifted in my mind—an audible click, like a gate unlatching. Without warning, a flood of memories rushed out.

The cool, damp walls of a cave.

My stomach turning at the words of someone better left

forgotten. "You've grown up to be more beautiful than I could've ever imagined."

Reaching out for Liam in my realm, only to be hauled back into that awful cave before I could tell him where I was.

The repulsive voice of my captor telling me Ronan, Emilio, and Darius were dead.

Magic seeping into my limbs, unleashed from the stone surrounding me.

Asher, my fiery incubus, his hands sliding up my back as I writhed in his lap, his eyes as wild as his kiss.

The look of fear dawning in Jonathan's twisted gaze as I attacked him.

"Your blood and your soul, hunter. That's what I need..."

My eyes snapped open as the last wisps of fog dissipated from my mind. Jonathan had taken Asher and me prisoner, shot Asher full of deadly nanotech—an internal devil's trap. Though I didn't believe him, he'd told me in gruesome detail how he'd tormented and killed the others. That he wanted me to join him on his sick, demented quest.

That he wanted my power. My ability to raise beings from the dead.

Asher and I... We...

Heat rushed to my cheeks as *that* particular memory danced through my mind. Despite the circumstances of our imprisonment, being with him like that—tasting his kiss, feeling him inside me, shattering with white-hot pleasure at his touch...

I shivered at the memory. Sex with Asher... It'd saved him.

15

In some ways, maybe it'd saved me, too.

Asher had given me the strength to do what needed to be done, no matter what the cost. After that, I'd attacked Jonathan and ripped out his soul, feeling it burn through me...

Holy shit.

I gasped as the realization hit me full on. I was in the Shadowrealm. Trapped, just as Liam had warned—my eternal punishment for breaking the natural order and banishing a soul here against his will.

But... that didn't make sense. If I *was* trapped, that meant that I'd succeeded in bringing Jonathan's soul here. My memories might've been slow to return, but I was almost positive I hadn't passed through my magical realm this time, hadn't walked that long and twisty path to the rune gate that separated my place from the Shadowrealm. That's how it'd happened with Travis, the man who'd killed Bean in the alley—I'd dragged his soul to the gate, intending on bringing him through. The only reason he didn't end up banished was that Liam stepped in and helped me see it wasn't for the best. Not that time, anyway.

But now with Jonathan, it seemed I'd been deposited here directly. No magic realm, no rune gate, no last-minute chances to turn back.

A new realization hit me, as frightening as it was impossible.

It wasn't just my soul trapped here, but *all* of me. Some-how, I'd physically manifested—I could feel it in the heavy weight of my steps, the press of gravity on my body, the sting of the fresh wounds on my palm.

Jonathan's soul, which had burned like living fire inside me from the moment I'd taken it in, was no longer with me.

Gray...

I jumped to my feet and spun around, certain I'd heard my name, like a whisper on the hot, acrid wind.

"Hello?" I croaked out.

Get out of here, Gray...

I'd *felt* it that time. A presence, followed immediately by the familiar scent of strawberries-and-cream.

"Sophie?" I asked, my heart already lifting with hope.

Goosebumps rose on my arms, the magic inside me flaring hot. Beneath my poorly-wrapped feet, the earth warmed, steam slithering out from hundreds of tiny cracks and crevices in the rock.

I closed my eyes, reaching out with my heart and mind and everything left inside me for any sign of Sophie, any way to connect with her.

An image flashed through my mind—but it wasn't my best friend. Instead, I saw a red demon with horns, a forked tail, and the dark wings of a fallen angel, hopping across a scorched patch of earth. Blood dripped from his teeth and claws, and his eyes blazed with raw hatred.

It was the Devil card from Sophie's tarot deck.

My eyes snapped open, but there was nothing around me but rock and smoke.

Move, Gray. Now...

Quickly, I readjusted my makeshift shoes and resumed

my trek along the ridge, fighting off the dizziness that threatened to overtake me. I was dehydrated, and the magic which had unlocked my memories was now buzzing impatiently through my body, seeking an outlet.

And someone was trying to warn me. I couldn't see her, but I could hear her. Feel her.

Faster, Gray...

"Soph?" My cracking voice echoed.

The only response I got was a breath of hot air, ash blowing into my eyes.

I blinked rapidly, slowing my steps against the rapidly increasing wind. It made my eyes water, and I had to stop completely until the burning passed.

When I opened my eyes again, two red demons stood on the path ahead of me, grinning wickedly, their sharp teeth glinting. I blinked rapidly, trying to dispel the hallucination, but the monsters only got closer.

I wasn't imagining them.

I spun around in search of an escape, but another appeared on the path where I'd just come from. I stood in shocked horror as it unfurled its tattered, leathery wings. It hopped from one foot to the other, flames licking up from the earth wherever its cloven foot touched.

There was nowhere to run.

Here in the in-between, where I was cursed to spend eternity, the devil card had come to life.

Shielding my face from the wave of heat that crested before me, I took a deep, ashy breath, calling on the magic still flickering inside me. I felt it warming inside me again, gearing up for whatever came my way, but it wasn't enough.

The hellish creatures had some major home-field advantage. They were fire demons, and I was pretty sure this entire realm was wrapped around a core of living flame. They seemed to be drawing power from it, their eyes glowing a bright orange-red as the flames at their feet grew hotter.

Before this moment, the closest I'd ever come to working with fire magic was the night at the safe house when I'd scried and connected with Reva through the flames.

I had no idea if I could wield it, but I didn't have a choice. I needed fire.

I closed my eyes and took a breath, envisioning my magic seeping out through my feet and into the rock below. I felt it penetrate the dense stone, working down to the molten core.

An image of a great underground inferno appeared in my mind's eye, and I held onto it, coaxing the flames higher as I whispered a final plea.

> *Spark, smoke, fire, inferno*
> *Burn here above as you burn down below*
> *Let rock join flame and fight as one*
> *Hear my words, let it be done*

Heat radiated up through my legs, the fire magic joining with my own.

It's working!

I channeled the magic into a burst of energy, watching it spark to life between my palms. Blue flames ignited in my hands.

And then I braced myself for the fight from hell.

THREE

DARIUS

In thirty-three years of life as a mortal and countless more as a vampire, I had known a great many liars.

Blood had never been one of them.

"Gray!" I gasped as the sudden rush of heat flooded my chest, followed by the sweet, heady scent of the witch who thoroughly owned my heart. The sensations were unmistakeable—the siren call of Gray's blood resurfacing after its days-long absence, more intense than it'd ever been before.

It was our blood bond. Sensing her this way... I swallowed the emotion tightening my throat. It meant she was still with us. Still alive.

I grabbed my cell phone, fumbling with the damn screen for several frustrating moments before I finally managed to punch in Ronan's number.

While he and Emilio were out at the Landes property hunting down clues, I'd been forced to wait out the daylight in a dank, moldering motel on the outskirts of

Raven's Cape, rendered nearly impotent by my deadly aversion to the sun. It'd been several hours and I'd yet to hear from either of them; I had to assume my connection to Gray was the first real spark of hope we'd received.

But before the second ring on Ronan's line, my hope died. The warmth that had buoyed my spirits only moments ago vanished just as quickly as it'd arrived, leaving a cold, hollow dread in its wake.

Something was wrong.

I closed my eyes and reached out for her with everything I had, following the tendrils of her scent that still lingered faintly. I could feel the rush of blood to her head. I could feel her fucking heartbeat.

It was too fast.

I forced myself to take another breath through my nose, my senses still hunting for more. Her presence came back stronger for a moment, but then soured. I felt things—*tasted* things—that simply should not have been. The surge of her magic, familiar but for a new tinge of something rotten and diseased. The sharp, knife-blade edge of her panic, followed almost at once by a flood of boundless determination. And though our blood bond did not afford me a glimpse into Gray's thoughts, my gut—which, much like blood, had never led me astray—told me that my little brawler was embarking on a journey from which she'd likely not return.

Ronan's voicemail greeting announced his absence, and I forced myself not to throw my damn phone into the wall.

Infernal damn devices!

"Vacarro," I barked. "Where the bloody hell are you?

Kindly return my call at your earliest convenience, by which I clearly mean call me back in the next two minutes unless you want to die a painful and bloody death the likes of which your kind has not yet known."

I tossed the phone onto the bed and paced the depressing room. Counted the unidentifiable stains in the dingy, threadbare carpet. Left three additional voicemails and sent a dozen texts to each of their numbers, none of which were being returned.

Bloody *hell*, waiting was a terrible way to pass the time.

Where could they possibly be?

Out of range? Stealthily tracking a potential source? In trouble?

Concern flickered in my gut as the last possibility continued to rear its ugly head.

I retrieved the phone.

"You've got one more minute, demon," I said, attempting to leave yet another pointless voicemail. "Or I'll have no choice but to—"

My warning was cut off by the flood of a new scent cresting just outside my door—adrenaline, mingled with fear and the unmistakable scent of raw male aggression. *Human* male aggression—the worst sort there was.

No sooner had I darted behind a tall dresser just inside the door did the keycard reader beep, and two brawny men slipped inside my room, quietly shutting the door behind them. They were fairly nondescript, dressed in plain jeans and faded T-shirts. Each had what appeared to be a rune branded into his inner forearm, but otherwise no identifiable tattoos or markings.

I was certain I'd never seen or scented them before. Yet they seemed to be looking for me. They'd procured a copy of my key.

And a set of dangerously pointy hawthorn stakes.

I had approximately eight more seconds before their eyes adjusted to the darkness of the room and they turned and spotted me.

The one who seemed to be in charge pointed at the Queen-sized bed at the center of the room, then gestured for the other to look underneath, as if they were dealing with a small child hiding from a monster.

At this, I grinned, my anxiety somewhat loosening.

I am the monster, you bloody imbeciles.

I supposed I owed the legends my gratitude; of the humans who believed in our existence, many thought we slept away the daylight hours in coffins. The dark, confined space under the bed seemed like the logical choice.

I'd be more than happy to set the record straight.

As the boss scanned the rest of the room, his number two—younger, probably less experienced—crouched down on the far side of the bed, stake clutched menacingly in his hand, and I saw my opportunity.

With all the strength I possessed, I shoved the tall dresser, plowing it into the boss and crushing him against the wall. I heard the crunch of bone and a deep grunt. The wet stain of his blood darkened the carpet below.

"Fuck!" Number Two shouted, leaping to his feet. "Jerry!"

"I'm afraid Jerry can't respond right now," I said. "Pity."

He stared at the stain on the carpet beneath the dresser. He was so disturbed by the sight, he seemed to have forgotten I was the cause of it.

Graceful as a cat, I launched myself over the bed and into his immediate space. I grabbed him by the throat and slammed him against the wall, his feet several inches off the ground. He snapped out of his stupor and attempted to put up a fight, but his youthful scrappiness did not avail him, and I disarmed him easily.

He was useless without his stake, offering no more than sputtering moans as I repeatedly pounded my fist into his face.

Bones shattered. Teeth dislodged. Skin tore. Blood glistened.

So. Much. Blood.

In a feeble attempt to block the onslaught, he raised shaky arms. The brand on his inner arm was streaked with blood, shining darkly in the dim room.

That rune...

Something about it tugged at my memory, but I couldn't quite place the image. Had I seen it before? A book, perhaps? Something of Gray's?

I grabbed his arm and wrenched it closer for a better look.

Something of Gray's...

Recognition slammed into me like a fist. I *had* seen it

before—the night Gray and I snuck into the morgue. It was an exact match for one of the symbols carved into the flesh of Blackmoon Bay's murdered witches.

Carved into Gray's best friend, Sophie.

Gray had only seen a photograph of it, but I'd never forget the sight of her face when she'd looked up at me across that room, pale and shaken. Utterly undone by the evidence of such gruesome torture.

I clenched my teeth, seething.

Jerry and his number two weren't just a pair of thugs keen on taking out an out-of-town vampire. They were witch hunters. And they knew we were here.

They'd either seen Ronan and Emilio drop me off before dawn, or someone in the motel's employ was connected to them. However they'd learned about my arrival in Raven's Cape, these men had come here to execute me in my sleep, assuming I'd be an easy kill.

My vision swam with red.

I slammed my fist into the wall beside his head, punching a crater into the plaster and brick. Unlike his friend Jerry, this guy was still breathing, and he gasped. Barely.

"Please," he whispered, the broken cry of a broken man who'd already stepped one foot through hell's gate.

"You don't deserve to beg, you fucking coward."

Some part of me—a faraway voice in my head—knew I should keep him alive for questioning. They were witch hunters, and they'd come to kill me. Likely they were connected to Jonathan, and they might've had information about Gray's whereabouts.

But the cool, rational part of me that had kept things running smoothly for decades was no more than a dim voice of protest, trapped behind a wall of red-hot rage.

I let out a roar, my unfiltered anger mixing with the scent of his adrenaline-spiked blood to ignite something feral inside me—something I'd kept chained up for far too long.

It was against Council law for me to take an unwilling victim. Against human law for me to kill him.

But for the first time in many, many years, I no longer cared about protocol. My body, which had learned over the decades to be satisfied with the chilled donor blood procured from medical establishments with poor security, suddenly vibrated with a deep, ancient need.

I was… *thirsty*.

I bent my head to his neck and opened my mouth. The room dimmed around me, all other concerns vanishing. There were only two things now that mattered: my rapidly-elongating fangs and his pulsing vein, begging to be pierced.

I bit into his flesh, enjoyed his gasp of shock.

I drank deeply. Desperately.

Warm, wet liquid filled my mouth, coating my throat. There was an angry, bitter tang to it, like wine that had long ago turned, but I didn't stop. Not even when my head spun and my skin buzzed with too much, too soon, too… everything.

Not even when I felt the last of his life force fade away.

I drained him quickly. Completely. Abandoned his life-less body without another thought.

Moving to the front of the room, I tipped the ruined dresser onto its side and peeled the other dead man from the wall.

So much blood... So thirsty...

I tossed his still-warm body onto the bed and climbed on top of him, wrenching his head back to expose the thick, corded veins of his neck.

I still had the wherewithal to understand I was heading down the path of darkness, but I chased that blackness eagerly, letting it fuel me. Fulfill me. Just as I'd done to his companion, I pierced his flesh and let the blood flow. His was even more bitter, but I was no longer concerned with taste.

I sucked greedily, ignoring the tremble rapidly spreading through my limbs.

A shallow grunting sound filled the room, much like an animal in heat, something wild and undignified. Moments later, with no more than a mild amusement touching my lips, I realized the animal was me.

I was spiraling, losing the last of the humanity I'd done my best to cling to for so many years. It would kill me, this indiscretion. We weren't made for this much blood at once; the overdose would surely wreck my mind, destroy my body, leave me comatose. Somewhere in the recesses of my mind I knew that, but it wasn't enough to make me stop.

How did I even get here?

Didn't matter. There was no point in considering the hows or whys. There was only thirst. Only drink. Only blood.

As I moved on to his wrist in search of a fresher vein, faintly I heard something—*sensed* something that gave me momentary pause. A whisper in my ear? A tingle creeping up my spine? A pinch of anxiety in my chest as if I'd forgotten something important?

I closed my eyes. Inhaled deeply.

Had I been... looking for something? Waiting? For someone? For...

Drink.

Dismissing the feeling, I sucked the dead man's flesh until my lips were sealed tight against it. Took a deep, dark drink. And let the world spin away from me one last time.

There was an image—no more than a flicker, really. The soft, silky touch of a woman's hair in my hands, her mouth on mine, the whisper of my name on her breath...

Darius...

I tried to hold onto it. To her.

But she slipped away, and everything around me went as black as the beast inside.

FOUR

GRAY

I forced the magic out through my palms, directing it at the two demons rushing toward me. The fireball exploded on impact, blasting them backward.

Another demon lunged at me from behind, spitting fire. I barely registered the burns, the pain. I retaliated with another fiery pulse that slammed into his chest and sent him reeling.

Their chilling screeches echoed across the otherworldly landscape.

But too quickly, the flames engulfing them died out. Their flesh remained unburnt.

Shit.

Other than buying me some time, my magic wasn't working on them, but theirs sure as hell worked on me. The skin on my arm was already black and blistering.

It seemed I was weaponless.

A demon struck my back with his whiplike tail, tearing through my shirt and splitting the skin beneath. Another raked his claws along my thigh, but they were holding back now—toying with me. Who knew how long this game would last.

Calling on my earth magic, I envisioned a curtain of rock surrounding me. I pictured it in my mind, willing it to manifest.

Suddenly, the loose rock and scree along the ridge rumbled and shot toward me in a swarm of dust and debris, encircling me in a protective silo.

It was dark inside, save for the faint red glow squeezing through the gaps between the jagged rocks.

It was crazy. This strange, inhospitable landscape was responding to my magic in ways that pushed the boundaries of my imagination—ways I'd never before experienced. It felt like a lucid dream. Like I could literally bend and shape and recreate the world by thought and intention alone.

A smile touched my tight-pressed lips.

This is how it should always be.

The magic inside me pulsed. My body buzzed with power.

But the demons outside my newfound walls weren't deterred. They hit me with a coordinated, sustained attack, their flames heating up the stones around me.

Immediately the temperature inside my silo began to rise.

They're going to cook me alive.

I was weakening fast, my muscles cramping, pain hammering my skull as my mind fought to hold on to the magic keeping the rocks in place.

And it was so. Fucking. Hot.

A few months ago, I might've tried to fight them. But I wasn't that crazy, impulsive witch anymore. I knew when I was outgunned, and I had no intention of becoming a human barbecue.

With one final, desperate burst of magical will, I blasted apart my stone silo, turning my protective rocks into projectiles that shot outward at my foes.

The demons were thrown back by the explosion, battered with a barrage of hot, sharp rocks.

Taking advantage of the momentary chaos, I threw myself down the rocky slope.

I tumbled forever, feeling every bump on the way down. When I finally stopped rolling, landing unceremoniously in a shallow depression at the bottom of the rise, I was pretty sure I'd died somewhere along the way.

But I wasn't dead. I could still feel every ache, every scrape. My skin was shredded, my bones rattling, my insides jumbled up like beaten eggs. And the fire demons had already taken wing—they were circling overhead.

Wincing, I pushed myself up and got to my feet, trying to get my bearings. The scent of sulfur was much stronger down here, but beneath it, I caught a faint strawberry whiff once again.

"Sophie?" My heart was pounding. Was she really here with me? "Where are you?"

Here, the voice responded. It sounded like it was inside me. *Come with me.*

"I can't see you!"

This way. Here, Gray. Hurry!

The response was louder this time, accompanied by a flash of coppery red—her hair blowing in the breeze.

"Hey!" I called out. "Wait!" I darted after the blur of colors ahead of me, catching a brief glimpse of her white lace tee and black miniskirt—completely out of place in this twisted realm—and those unmistakable red curls.

Curls that flickered with rainbow light.

I laughed as I jogged after her, ignoring the pain, the burn in my lungs, the ash filling my mouth. Smoke billowed across the landscape, winding its way around me as the demons circled closer, but my Sophie was here, and I pressed on.

I couldn't lose her. Not in this awful place.

"Sophie! Wait!" I'd reached the edge of another rocky rise, but unlike the steep drop from the ridge, this one descended gradually. At the bottom, not too far in the distance, the landscape morphed into a lush, inviting forest that I could've sworn wasn't there before.

It made no sense, but I didn't care. A cool breeze drifted up from the woods, rolling across the valley and up to greet me. In front of me, for as far as the eye could see, the earth was green and verdant, teeming with life. That meant there was a water source. Probably food—edible plants, maybe even a rabbit or deer.

My mouth watered at the thought.

Sophie was waiting for me down below, frantically waving from a copse of ponderosa pine, the ground at her feet blanketed in pink and white flowers.

I zipped down the slope, desperate to reach her. But the closer I got, the more transparent she became.

She was fading away, and we hadn't even gotten the chance to talk.

"Sophie, wait!" I called out. "Don't go!"

But it was too late. By the time I reached the woods, she'd vanished entirely.

Had she even been here at all? Maybe it was just a vivid hallucination brought on by my fatigue and dehydration.

I sagged against one of the ponderosa pines, breathing in the sweet, butterscotch aroma of its bark. At least I was out of the heat.

The forest ahead was silent—a calm oasis in this harsh, inhospitable place. I turned to look over my shoulder, hoping the demons hadn't seen me slip into the woods. But they were nowhere in sight. None of it was. The fiery, barren land I'd been traversing for days was just… gone. Behind me was more forest, stretching on for miles and miles.

The Shadowrealm was much more vast and complex than I'd ever imagined.

Whether or not Sophie's spirit had guided me here, I figured I might as well continue on in the direction I was heading. I took a step forward, clearing the copse of ponderosa.

The sight before me nearly brought me to my knees.

Surrounded by the same pink and white flowers I'd seen beneath the trees, a serene, glassy lake glistened ahead, beckoning me forward.

With a burst of renewed hope, I jogged over to the edge and waded in up to my ankles, then my knees, tears of gratitude stinging my eyes as the cool, healing water soothed my damaged skin. Inch by inch I sank down, squishing my toes into the muddy bottom, letting the waterline graze my lips.

It was a struggle not to gulp it all in, but I didn't want to get sick. I sipped it slowly, letting the water replenish me. It was clean and pure and cool, but unlike water out of the tap back home, this had other properties.

Maybe it was another trick, maybe even one more dangerous than a hallucination, but I *felt* the water healing my wounds, my skin tingling as it knit itself back together. Inside, the water quenched my thirst, filling me up and giving me strength. The hunger that had gnawed holes into my stomach faded into a dull ache hardly worth noticing. And everything in my mind sharpened, clarified.

Feeling renewed, I leaned backward and floated effortlessly, gazing up at the sky. No longer dark and miserable, it was a stunning sapphire blue, bright and cloudless. There was no sun that I could see, but everything about it felt like a sunny, beautiful day.

I could stay here forever, just floating…

I relaxed my arms and legs, my eyelids growing heavy. A gentle breeze kissed my cheeks, carrying with it the scents of lavender and lilac. The combination seemed familiar to me, but I couldn't quite place it. My mother's perfume, maybe? A garden from my childhood?

No matter. I didn't need to know. Or remember. Or think. Or exist.

I just needed to drift. Drift away like smoke on the breeze. Or maybe I would just become water. It was already happening—I could feel it, cell by cell, starting in my toes. They were disappearing into the lake. My legs would be next. Then my torso. My arms. Everything.

I should've been frightened, or at least startled, but I wasn't.

This... this was meant to be. I'd found my place. My purpose.

Mindlessly, I began to chant, whispering the mantra as if I'd heard it a thousand times.

I am the water, the water is me

I am the water, the water is me

I am the water

Water

Water

Water...

No, Gray... You're lingering too long. You can't!

Water water water water...

Wake up. Wake up now! Gray! GRAY!

I gasped at the sound of Sophie's voice, yanking me out of my haze. My eyes snapped open, and I dropped through the water like a stone, sputtering as it filled my mouth.

It tasted like rot.

I swam to the shore and dragged myself out, shivering. Behind me, the lake turned menacing, the water suddenly black and murky as mist rolled over the surface. It'd come out of nowhere, filling the entire forest.

I was completely disoriented, scared to move for fear of ending up back in the lake.

"What now?"

I was hoping Sophie would answer. Instead, the magic inside me warmed, and I felt a gentle tug, like someone was pulling on a string connected to my bellybutton.

Trusting it, I followed in the direction of the pull.

After only a minute or two of walking, the mist parted. Several yards ahead, I spotted the edge of a new forest, barren and eerie, with black, leafless trees draped with black-and-silver threads.

My heart leaped. I'd know those trees anywhere—they were part of the black forest that now surrounded my magical realm. Part of my realm, according to Liam. Part of the source of my power.

My magic stirred again, tugging me forward as if it were being called home. Hope surged inside me. Maybe I wasn't trapped. If I could get back to my own magic realm, I could find Liam. I could find a way back to the material plane. Back to my rebels.

The trees seemed to be welcoming me as I approached,

stretching out their black branches, their silver tinsel fingers fluttering in the breeze.

Mesmerized, I reached out to touch them, eager to get back to my realm. My palms glowed indigo as the silver threads wrapped around my fingers in a gentle caress, urging me forward.

Urging me home.

I took my first step into the black forest.

I was home. So, so close I could taste it, the lilac and lavender scent of my sacred place filling me so completely, it almost felt as if I'd never left. Not even after Calla died.

It'd been a long time since I'd felt so happy. So relieved.

And then I froze.

A heavy hand fell on my shoulder from behind, its grip tightening painfully.

"Leaving the shadows already, Sunshine?" His voice slithered down my spine, so close I could feel his damp breath on the back of my neck.

I turned to face him. My captor. My tormentor. The man I'd loved more than a decade ago. The man who led his family to my house to butcher the only mother I'd ever known.

The one I'd sentenced to an eternity in this place, just as I'd sentenced myself.

"Haven't you had enough of this, Jonathan?" I jerked away from his touch, but he grabbed me again, his fingers digging into my flesh. He had no fingernails left.

"Let me go," I said. "Or I'll—"

"Or you'll what? Rip out my soul and banish me to the

Shadowlands?" He grinned, most of his teeth missing now, the dead-animal stench of his breath turning my stomach. "I'm afraid that plan didn't work out so well. So now we're gonna do things according to *my* plan. And Sunshine? You're not going to like it one bit."

FIVE

EMILIO

My gun and badge were missing.

I opened my eyes and sat bolt upright, and was swiftly rewarded with a lancing pain through my skull, so bright and sharp I nearly puked.

Clutching my head in my hands, I squeezed my eyes shut and waited for the nausea to pass. It cleared out fast enough, only to pave the way for another shot of pain. This one, however, brought a rush of memories back with it— Leaving Darius at the motel. Ronan and I searching for clues at the Landes place, where Gray's ex had left us a message in the form of a body wearing her mother's amulet. The two of us getting ambushed by the local pack, headed up by none other than the Raven's Cape Chief of Police, Elena Alvarez.

My sister.

Damn.

I blew out a breath. At least she hadn't killed us. From

the looks of things, she'd brought us back to her place. I was on a leather couch in the living room, a bright, airy space with gleaming wood floors, lots of windows, and cheerful yellow-orange walls.

As nice as it was, though, something didn't feel right about the place. It took me a minute to realize what it was.

There was nothing remotely personal about it. No photos. No knickknacks. The books on the shelves were decorative, and the sparsely-placed art on the walls was the kind of framed generic crap you could pick up at any department store.

Still, I knew it was my sister's place. I could feel her presence everywhere, and the color of the walls was the exact same shade my father had painted her bedroom in Mendoza when we were kids.

Tangerine sunset, it was called. He'd sent me back to the hardware store in town for more when he realized one coat wouldn't be enough.

Gingerly, I rose from the couch and stretched. My muscles were stiff and tight, my back cracking and creaking.

Shifters aged at about half the rate of humans and lived three times as long, but hell. Even with such a long life ahead of me, I still felt like I was getting old.

At least my head had stopped throbbing.

I looked around and got my bearings. I was alone in the tangerine sunset room, but Ronan was around here some-where—his scent was fresh, as was the recently brewed coffee and something that smelled a lot like Mamá's *tortilla de papas.*

If I let myself, I could almost pretend we were back home. That all the people we'd so fiercely loved—the pack —were still alive. That everything had turned out differently.

But that had never done me a damn bit of good.

So I went with anger instead.

"Elena!" I roared her name, the sound of it still foreign and gritty in my ears. "*Elena!*"

"Well, well!" came her sarcastic reply. "The lone wolf lives."

She stepped out from behind a pair of French doors at the other end of the room, arms crossed over her chest, dark hair spilling over her shoulders. Now that she wasn't pointing a gun at my chest, I took a minute to take in the sight of her. She was thinner than I remembered, but muscular, dressed in jeans and black v-neck tank top that showed off her well-defined arms. She had a long, narrow nose and sharp cheekbones that'd always made her look both beautiful and intimidating. But time hadn't softened the severity of her face. Just the opposite; there were lines around her mouth and a streak of gray in her hair that hadn't been there the last time I'd seen her.

Her eyes were just like mine.

I couldn't look away.

She cocked her hip and leaned against the doorframe, piercing me with her intense gaze as if she were daring me to start trouble.

I almost laughed.

Decades vanished in a blink, and suddenly I was a kid again, sipping *maté* on our front porch in the Mendoza foothills, grinning at my big sister like I knew all her secrets. She was supposed to have been on a camping trip with her girlfriends, but her boyfriend had just dropped her off, and I'd caught them making out in his car. It was clear she'd spent the weekend with him.

Mamá would've skinned her alive if she'd found out. Not because she'd lied and snuck off with a boy—my parents were pretty liberal about things like that.

It was because my sister was the alpha fated to lead our pack, and that boy was human.

You can't tell on me, Meelo. You'll ruin everything!

I extorted the hell out of her that summer. Got fifty bucks for my silence, which was basically a million dollars in my kid mind.

But in the end, her secret cost her a hell of a lot more than that.

I cleared my throat, trying to swallow the knot that'd suddenly lodged there.

"How long was I out?"

"A few hours. Ronan came to about an hour ago."

"Care to explain the welcome gift?" I snapped, rubbing the fresh lump on my head. I had to stay mad at her. The moment I let that anger slip away, the moment I let the memories take hold of me, the guilt would rush in and eat me alive. "And give me back my weapon, while you're at it. Unless you'd like me to get in touch with your supervisor."

She pressed her lips together and sighed loudly through her nose, but she retrieved my gun from on top of the tall china cabinet behind her. A wave of her scent hit me as she approached, tightening the knot in my throat.

I held my breath until it passed. Nostalgia never helped anyone. It just confused the hell out of us, making us believe we could travel through time on a scent, on a song, on a smile. Making us believe we could go back and fix all the fucked-up shit we'd done to each other.

Even in this crazy world of witches and vampires and shifters and magic, life just didn't work that way.

Handing over the weapon, she said, "It was for your own protection, Emilio. If you can't see that—"

"You knocked me out. Left me with a hell of a headache, too. Maybe even a concussion."

Ronan laughed. "Toughen up, wolf pup."

I growled at him. Fucking traitor. What the hell had he and my sister been chatting about for the last hour, anyway? They should've woken me up.

"How did we even get here?" I snapped. "Did you wake up with a headache, too?"

Ronan rubbed the side of his head and winced. "Yeah. One of her wolf pups got me good. Then they threw us in the back of the van and brought us here."

"Where are these wolf pups now?" I asked.

"My *men* are out working the Landes case." Elena shook her head. "It's not them you're mad at. It's me. They were just following orders."

"Orders to assault an officer of the law and his companion?"

Elena lifted her shoulder in the most casual shrug I'd ever seen. "So you'd rather be dead than pop a few aspirin?"

"You should've warned me, not cold-cocked me."

"There was no time to explain." She headed to the windows that overlooked the backyard, peering out into the daylight. When she spoke again, her voice was heavy with worry. "This whole town is crawling with dark fae and human outsiders we're pretty sure are witch hunters. If they'd found you snooping around the Landes place, they would've either killed you or taken you, and who knows what—."

"Hunters and dark *fae*?" I followed her to the window and grabbed her elbow, forcing her to turn around and face me. "Christ, Elena. When we spoke on the phone about the Landes murder, you told me there hadn't been any witch killings or other supernatural crimes in the area."

"There *haven't* been." She jerked her arm out of my grasp. "Just the Landes case, which we still haven't solved. For all we know, it was a spurned ex. We can't prove the out-of-towners are hunters, and until they make a move on any of our witches, we can't charge them with anything but the occasional speeding ticket or drunk and disorderly. And last time I checked, it's not illegal to be dark fae."

"Yet you felt they were dangerous enough to warrant knocking Ronan and me out without explanation for our own good?" I shook my head. Fucking Elena. Leave it to my sister to keep me in the dark about something so important. "You're truly unbelievable, Elena."

A familiar fire blazed in her eyes. "Forgive me, brother, for not keeping you abreast of the population demographics of Raven's Cape. Would you like a tour through our case files, while we're at it? How about the keys to the city?"

"Stop. Just... Listen to me." I grabbed her chin and tipped her face up, refusing to back down from her steely gaze. Keeping my tone as measured as possible, I said, "Whatever your feelings for me, you need to put that aside. People's lives are at stake. Our cases are overlapping here, and something tells me the violence and mayhem we're experiencing in the Bay is just the tip of the iceberg."

"What do you want from me, Emilio?"

"I want you to be straight with me. That's it. Keeping secrets is liable to get a lot more people killed."

Fire still lit her eyes, but her shoulders relaxed, and she blew out a soft breath. In a softer voice, she said, "You wouldn't have listened to me, anyway. You never have."

I opened my mouth to argue, but even after all our years apart, no one knew me like Elena.

I wouldn't have listened. Not until it was too late.

I sat back down on the couch and blew out a breath. My sister may have spent the last twenty years dreaming about my death, but she'd made one thing clear: when it came down to it, she didn't really *want* me to die. Despite her caginess, she was trying to help us.

The thought was more comforting than I wanted to

admit.

"I want to know what's going on," I said, forcing my voice to remain calm. Escalating things would only waste time—time we needed to track down Gray and Asher. "You owe me that much."

It was the wrong thing to say.

A sliver of laughter escaped her lips, cold and sharp as those killer cheekbones. "So now we're talking about settling debts? That's rich."

Shame burned in my gut, twisting me inside out. Ghosts of the past tried their best to pry their way out of the box I'd locked them away in, but I grit my teeth against their onslaught, forcing them back inside. We'd had twenty years to sift through the relics of the past, but we'd wasted it avoiding each other instead, and now there was no time to reminisce.

"Our friends are missing—witches from Blackmoon Bay and the surrounding areas," I said. "We have reason to believe they're being held captive somewhere in Raven's Cape."

"What reason might that be?"

I looked across the room to Ronan, who'd remained mostly silent throughout the conversation. How could we explain all of this to her? Where did we even start? Gray's scrying? The amulet? Everything the Grinaldi-sired vampire, Fiona, had confessed about Jonathan's twisted plans? It was too much to get into.

"You're just gonna have to trust me," I said.

"Not happening."

"Elena—"

"Not. Happening." She folded her arms in front of her chest and raised an eyebrow. I wasn't surprised. Elena was as stubborn as they came. The entire world could be burning around us, and she'd wait me out until her hair caught fire.

Maybe even longer than that.

Still, she was right not to trust me.

Everyone she loved was dead because of me.

I leaned my head back, staring up at the ceiling. We needed the cooperation of the RCPD, or we'd never get off the ground in this town. Gray and Asher—along with Haley, Reva, and countless others—didn't have much time.

Elena had backed me into a corner, and I had no recourse but to give in.

"Okay," I finally said. "I'll tell you what I know. But it's a long story, and like I said, people's lives are at stake. Innocent people, including at least one teenage girl."

Elena gasped. "Fair enough. You share your info, then I'll tell you what we know, too. Agreed?"

"Agreed."

"See? Was that so hard?" she asked, and I swore I felt her smug smile beaming at me from across the room. "Let me put on some fresh coffee while you clean up."

"Clean up?"

"No offense, wolf," she said with a wink, "but you smell like you spent the morning passed out in the back of a van."

I laughed. It was the kindest thing she'd said to me in twenty years.

SIX

EMILIO

My sister made a phone call, and fifteen minutes later, two of the three shifter detectives that had put Ronan and me into sleep mode appeared on her doorstep.

Ronan and I had just finished briefing Elena on all of the pertinent information about Gray and the ongoing supernatural crime wave in Blackmoon Bay—*pertinent* being the operative word. I saw no reason to bring up Gray's Shadowborn powers and her relationship with Death.

Darius had notified Liam about Gray's disappearance, but we hadn't heard from him since. I had no idea if he'd been in touch with her—or just *out* of touch with us.

I hoped it was the former. Just because we couldn't trace Gray didn't mean she was totally alone. If Liam could sense her—if he could connect with her through their strange, otherworldly bond—he might be able to help her.

The thought buoyed me.

And for Elena's part, all indications were that she'd

uphold her end of the deal and help us pool our resources on this.

I could've done without the two big wolves looming over us, but we needed the intel, and if that's how my sister wanted to roll, we'd play it her way.

For now.

"Boys," she said, "meet Detectives Aiden Hobb and Russel Lansky, my right-hand men. Detectives, meet the boys of Blackmoon Bay. Ronan Vacarro and..." She looked at me and hesitated, weighing her words before finally settling on the truth. "My brother, Detective Emilio Alvarez."

She'd said the word *brother* like she'd just bitten into a lemon, but at least she hadn't tried to pass me off as someone else.

"You've got a mean right hook," I said, shaking Hobb's hand. For the sake of the investigation and a shot at saving our friends, I was willing to overlook the assault. I even smiled to let him know there weren't any hard feelings.

Hobb shook my hand, but he clearly wasn't interested in my humor. Or my smile. Or anything even remotely human. He held tight a few seconds longer than necessary, sizing me up the whole time. Aggression and distrust rolled off him in waves.

"Thanks for coming over," I said, hoping to ease the tension. "We appreciate the cooperation on this."

His grip tightened, and he arched an eyebrow. We were about the same height, with similar builds, but now he lifted his chin and peered down at me, as if he needed to feel taller than me. Better. "Who said anything about cooperation?"

I squeezed his hand right back and grinned.

I had no intention of submitting—I had no loyalty to him, and he'd yet to earn my respect—but I wasn't about to challenge him outright, either. Like it or not, the RC was his territory. Ronan and I were outsiders, and Hobb wanted us to know it.

A pack of lone wolves didn't have the same structure as a traditional pack, where one alpha typically led. Wherever he'd come from, this guy was clearly an alpha, but so was my sister—and she was his boss. They seemed to make it work, but I was betting it hadn't been an easy ride for either of them. Alphas butted heads a lot, and the power dynamics were a minefield—one of the many reasons I'd kept to myself after Elena and I parted ways.

In one last attempt at camaraderie, I kept my grin in place and said calmly, "We'd like to tell you what we've been dealing with in the Bay. If you guys have got any insights, we'd love to hear them. No obligations beyond that. Fair enough?"

He offered a stiff nod. Apparently, that was as friendly as this guy got.

The other shifter was much warmer, with a youthful smile and an easy-going nature—clearly the good cop in this operation.

"Don't worry about Hobb," he said with a wink. "He's just pissed your sister keeps breaking up with his big dumb ass."

"Guys." Elena sighed. "Can we *try* to keep things professional for one day? Just one? Please?"

"You two are a thing?" I asked, gesturing between them.

"One date! One!" she exclaimed, and Hobb grunted out something that almost passed for a laugh. Smacking him in the chest, she said, "Hobb just doesn't know how to move on. So." She clapped once and nodded toward the dining room table. "If we're done with the awkward trip down memory lane, I'd really like to get down to business. That, and I'm starving."

There was no point in asking the rest of us. Wolves were always hungry, and Ronan wouldn't say no to food, either.

As we took our seats around the table, Elena served up strong curl-your-toes coffee and heaping plates of *tortilla* and fruit salad while I tried to avoid my own trip down memory lane.

Ronan brought her men up to speed, carefully skirting the same details I had about Gray's other powers and her connection to Death.

"So *that's* why you requested the amulet from forensics," Lansky said when Ronan had finished.

I nodded, spearing a strawberry with my fork. "It belonged to Gray's mother. It was taken from her long ago by the father of the hunter we're tracking."

"And?" Hobb asked.

"And we'd like to return it to its rightful owner," Ronan said. His face was a mask of steel, but his leg was bouncing under the table. He was just as anxious as I was to get on with the show—to get out there and do something.

Unfortunately, it looked like we'd have to endure more of this dog-and-pony show first.

"Out of the goodness of your hearts?" Hobb drained his coffee cup, then let out a grunt. "So tell me, how long *have* you two been fucking the little *bruja*?"

Ronan and I were out of our chairs in a flash, but Lansky jumped in first.

"Lay off, asshole," he barked at Hobb. "We all want the same thing here—to keep our communities safe and out of the spotlight. The sooner you drop the chip on your shoulder, the sooner we can get back to doing our jobs."

"Couldn't have said it better myself." Elena shot Hobb an icy glare before heading into the adjoining kitchen to refill the coffee carafe. "Hobb, this is your one and only warning. Reign it in, or see yourself out."

Hobb growled under his breath, but he lowered his eyes in submission to his Chief.

I wanted to bust his balls for giving in to her so easily, but we didn't have time for that shit. Instead, I said, "My gut tells me that whatever's going on in the Bay and the other super communities in the region—including Raven's Cape—can all be traced back to the same source."

"You're basing all this on a *hunch*?" Hobb said. "From everything you're telling us, other than the amulet and some visions in a fireplace, you haven't found *any* evidence that the witches are being held here."

This time, I *did* get out of my chair, shoving it back so hard it hit the wall and cracked the wainscoting. "Look, Hobb. I don't know what your problem is, but we've got our hands full here. We're talking about several murders, missing persons, a hostage situation, and a violent supernatural crime wave. If that's not enough to keep you awake at night, there's also intel from a source close to our hunter suggesting he's creating some sort of *super* supernatural army, hybridizing witches with vamps, shifters, demons, fae, you name it. So if lending a hand isn't your thing, fine. But do us all a favor—including the women and girls whose lives you're putting at risk with all this dick-swinging bullshit—and stop wasting our time."

His eyes glinted with malice, the low rumble in his throat turning into a growl. "Fuck you, wolf. You show up unannounced in *my* jurisdiction, giving—"

"Fuck me? Fuck *me*?" Forget keeping things smooth. I was done playing this guy's power games. I growled right back at him, my heart hammering, my muscles tensing for a fight.

Ronan got up and stood by my side, his eyes demon-black. "Ever been to hell, Hobb? Because you're about one dick move away from earning your one-way ticket."

"That's enough," Elena said calmly, rolling her eyes as if we were no more than a pack of kids fighting over a toy in the sandbox. Maybe that was the life of an alpha among alphas, but I wasn't used to this kind of pushback. "All of you, sit down and take a deep breath."

We glared at each other another beat, then finally took our seats again. This was my sister's home. Kicking her boyfriend's ass and destroying her dining room was probably not the best way to patch up our decades-old rift.

"Emilio," Elena said, "let's try to remember whose jurisdiction you're in. And Hobb—"

"Screw jurisdictions. I'm—"

"And *Hobb*," she continued, silencing my protests with her patented icy glare, "my brother is right. This affects us all, and it's *all* connected." She put a hand on Hobb's shoulder as she leaned over to refill his coffee cup—a quiet gesture that seemed to relax him. "There's no such thing as coincidence."

Her words lit a spark in my chest, reminding me of Gray. How many times had she said that very thing?

I took a sip of coffee to buy a second or two to myself. As a detective, I'd learned the importance of compartmentalizing, especially when I was working a case with personal stakes. I had to; I wouldn't be able to function otherwise. But now I closed my eyes and allowed myself a peek behind the wall—the one I'd so carefully erected to keep my personal feelings about Gray separate from my investigation of her disappearance. I pictured her face the moment she'd tasted my brownies, all blissed out and happy. The way she twirled her hair when she was reading her book of shadows, so lost in the pages she didn't even realize she was doing it. Her fierce determination when Darius and I had started training her to fight. The feel of her gentle touch when she'd kissed me on the cheek after I'd bought her new shampoo.

My chest hurt, but it was worth the pain. I needed to remember why I was sitting here dealing with Hobb and all the leftover shit between me and my sister. It was because

Gray was more important than my petty desires to avoid all of that discomfort, and the idea of anyone hurting her again...

My teeth clenched so tight, my jaw ached.

"We'll get her back, brother," Ronan whispered, pulling me out of my trance.

When I looked over at him, his eyes were no longer black, but full of the same pain I felt inside. In that moment, I realized he understood *exactly* where my mind had gone.

He understood it, because his own mind had never left that dark, tormented place. Not from the moment Gray was taken from us.

He'd loved her for a long time. I was just getting to know her again, but already I cared for her more than I could put into words. I couldn't even imagine how hard this must've been on him.

I didn't know how he handled the pain, the fear, but I only knew one way. So I slammed that wall firmly back into place and focused on the job, just like I'd done on every other horrible case I'd ever worked.

"No," Lansky said, "there isn't."

It took me a beat to realize he was still talking about coincidence.

"The amulet on its own is enough to link Gray's disappearance with the Landes murder," he went on, "but there's also Landes' van. They got it on camera when the hunter nabbed the incubus and the other witch, right? As far as we know, Landes himself is clean. And why else would hunters and fae be popping up in the RC if not to orchestrate something like this? We haven't had issues with them in a long time."

Everyone looked to Hobb, who finally blew out a breath and nodded.

"Yeah, alright," he said. "You guys have a point."

He didn't seem too thrilled about that fact, but I was ecstatic. After wasting the entire morning arguing and trying to make our case, it seemed we'd finally gotten everyone on the same page.

"Good." I tapped on the table, anxious to move forward. "Good. So let's start with the commonalities. If we can find the obvious connecting points, we might be able to fill in some of the gaps, see where—"

"It isn't *good*, Emilio." Elena's face paled, the lines around her mouth deepening. Standing there still clutching the coffee pot, her brow furrowed, she looked so much like our mother my heart stalled out.

"What's wrong?" I asked.

Elena headed back into the kitchen with the coffee pot. When she returned, she leaned against the wall and folded her arms over her chest, lowering her eyes like she didn't want to see my reaction.

For the first time since I'd woken up in her house, I sensed a hint of fear beneath her tough facade.

"The fae showing up in the RC?" she said, her voice a hell of a lot lower than it had been moments earlier. "They're Darkwinter."

Darkwinter? Now my stalled-out heart sank into my gut like a damn stone. I was no expert on Fae politics, but everyone knew the Darkwinter bloodline was the cruelest, most brutal, most frightening clan alive.

"How do you know it's them?" I asked. "Are you absolutely sure?"

She and Hobb exchanged a glance.

Hobb cleared his throat. "A confidential source—"

"A confidential *fae* source," Elena clarified. "She took a huge risk in coming forward, so don't bother asking for her name."

I let it go. I understood the importance of protecting sources, and the last thing I wanted was for anyone else to end up in the line of fire on this one—especially if Darkwinter were involved.

"Does your source have any idea what they're after?" Ronan asked. "Why they'd team up with hunters?" His leg was jumping again, the twitchy energy pulsing like an electrical field around his body. It made me want to punch something.

"It's clearly connected," Elena said, "But teaming up? I'm not so sure. Fae don't usually trouble themselves with rivalries between other supers, let alone human hunters and witches. Maybe the fae and the hunters are working different angles here."

Ronan shook his head. "No coincidences, remember?"

"No, I suppose not." She leaned her head back against the wall and closed her eyes, the scent of her fear cresting.

Hobb rose from his chair and headed into the kitchen, casually brushing his fingers against her bare arm as he passed. It happened so quickly, I almost hadn't seen it.

The scent of her fear instantly receded.

One date my ass.

"Ronan's right," I said, shifting my attention away from my sister and her alpha douchebag. Her relationships were none of my business—a lesson I should've learned a long fucking time ago.

"According to *our* sources," I continued, "the hunter we've been tracking is a rogue who split off from his family years ago. We already know he was working with vampires in the Bay—mercenary types looking to make a fast buck. And the way Gray disappeared? Time-release poison gas and a tracking device that could only be fae magic. So if you're telling us you've got a dark fae infestation in Raven's Cape, yeah, my money's on them. Looks like they're pinch-hitting for the hunters."

"If that's true," Lansky said, "there's gotta be something major in it for them."

"That's what I'm afraid of," I admitted. The known quantities were terrifying enough, but the deeper we dug, the clearer it became that we'd only just scratched the surface of this case.

"Okay," Elena said, looking at each of us in turn as she counted off on her fingers. "We've got missing and murdered witches, a missing rogue vampire with a personal connection to the prime suspect, a dead human, a likely hostage situation, hunters and fae skulking around Raven's Cape... It's a lot to process. Where does that leave us?"

Her eyes landed on me at that last question, and

everyone else seemed to understand that it was mine to answer.

What could I say? Elena and I might be estranged. Hell, she might hate me for the rest of her life. But in another lifetime, on another continent, we'd made a good team once. If that's what it took to keep our world safe, then we'd just have to make a good team again.

If not as pack, then as partners.

I stood up and thrust out my hand, hoping like hell she'd take it. "It leaves us partners."

Reluctantly, she nodded and grasped my hand, the familiar touch warm despite her hesitation. Her soft brown eyes were so like my own it felt like looking in a mirror, and the longer I stared at her, the deeper it hurt. Flashes of our shared childhood seemed to flicker in her gaze, and I wondered whether all those once happy memories were tainted for her now.

They weren't for me. They never would be, no matter what we'd done to each other.

Maybe, after all this shit was over, I'd find a way to tell her as much.

"Thank you, Elena." I released her hand and turned away before she sensed the swell of emotion in my chest. My sister and I had been estranged for twenty years, and that kind of rift didn't just vanish after one good meal and a handshake.

The past would have to wait. Right now I had to focus on—well—right now. And all that mattered right now was finding Gray and bringing her back home.

SEVEN

GRAY

The only warning I had was a tingling at the base of my neck and a gentle whisper inside my mind.

Duck.

Instinctively I dropped into a crouch, feeling the whoosh of air over my head as Jonathan swung his fist.

No way was I giving him another shot—I rocketed back up to my feet, simultaneously driving the heel of my hand into his nose.

The bone snapped. Blood gushed down his face.

Jonathan wailed and cradled his busted nose, but within seconds, he was coming at me again, his eyes crazed, his voice pitched high.

"You're nothing but a demon slut!" he shouted, taking another awkward swing. I dodged, easily pivoting away from him. He coughed and sputtered as the blood ran into his mouth, but that didn't stop him from hurling more insults. "You knocked me out so you could let him have his way with you, didn't you?"

He was talking about Asher, but I didn't respond—just let him keep shouting, tiring himself out.

"Just like he's having his way with all the other witches now that you're out of the picture," he ranted. "That's what incubuses do. How does that make you feel, whore?"

His comment didn't even register. I hoped Asher *had* found the others—if so, he was already working on a plan to rescue them, with Haley and Reva at his side. That was the picture that kept me going. The one that would carry me through my eternal sentence in this realm.

My friends would be safe, because Asher had made a promise. After all the fighting, the making up, the things that had and hadn't happened between us, I knew without a doubt he'd keep it.

That's what it meant to be a true friend. Looking out for each other. Keeping promises. Making sacrifices.

Jonathan didn't know anything about that.

He continued his endless babbling, but I refused to take the bait—just continued to duck and weave as we circled each other. For all his tough talk, he was rapidly deteriorating, panting heavily, sweat gleaming on his forehead, blood covering his face.

"It's me you want, Sunshine," he said. "Me you've always wanted."

At this, I finally spoke up. "It's you I want *dead*, Jonathan. There's a difference."

He continued on as if I hadn't said a thing. "I'm willing

to forgive your trickery back in the caves. You were upset. Confused. The demon had just sapped your energy, and you weren't in control of your own mind when you attacked me. Of course, witches are deceitful by nature, and curious too—a bad combination." He hobbled closer, more unsteady on his feet than he'd been even a minute ago. "All the more reason we mages must reclaim our birthright. The righteous among us will always rise above the wicked and depraved."

"Mages?" I rolled my eyes. "Save your hunter propaganda. Your preaching days are over."

"Not over," he spat. "Not by a long shot."

"Hunters are going extinct and you know it," I goaded. "That's why you're so desperate. You're the last generation of a dying breed that should've been put out of its misery long ago."

I had no intention of letting him get under my skin again, but Jonathan took *my* bait—hook, line, and sinker.

"We're evolving, witch," he snapped. "The old ways are dying, sure. But for those of us willing to embrace change? We'll survive. Just like we've always done. And we'll come out of this even stronger."

"You're not evolving. You're playing Dr. Frankenstein with a bunch of supers, hoping for a miracle. It won't work, Jonathan."

"Oh, but I've already seen results." He stopped circling me and grinned like a total psycho, revealing the blackened holes where most of his teeth used to be.

Though he'd manifested here physically just like I had,

his body seemed to be breaking down at a rapid pace. In addition to the nose job I'd given him, the wounds and imperfections I'd noticed back in the caves were even more pronounced now. Pieces of flesh had torn away from his face, revealing melon-colored wounds crusted with black blood. His hair was thin and patchy, and one of his eyes kept rolling to the side.

"Results, huh?" I let my gaze roam down to his feet, then back up again, locking on his deteriorating face. What the hell had he done to himself, anyway? "How's that working out for you?"

His eyes widened, glazing over as if he were dreaming of some great, golden laboratory in the sky where all of his dreams would one day come true, and his father would march in there and give him a trophy and a big, manly hug, and together they'd toss back a few beers, light some torches, and go burn down a village.

"It's not about me, Sunshine," he proclaimed. "Nope, nope, nope!"

He was pure insanity, a literal raving lunatic.

And I'd trapped myself here with him.

For. Ever.

"You claim witches can't be turned into vampires," he raved on, "but here's a little secret: one already has."

"You're so full of shit, Jonathan. Back in the caves, you told me you were working on it. Now it's a done deal?"

"We're just waiting on the final tests, but all indications are that it worked. And before you get all sanctimonious on me, she volunteered. Oh, yes, *that* witch knows about sacrifice for the greater good. And she was rewarded for her loyalty with more power you can even imagine."

I stilled, narrowing my eyes at him, trying to find the lie in his words. Jonathan read my silence as intrigue, stepping closer and offering a mad, bloody smile. But I wasn't intrigued at all. My brain was still stuck on the part about the witch who'd turned. Was that true, or just another one of his tricks? Witches never survived the vampire blood swap. So how had he done it? Fiona said he'd been *working* on technology to hybridize witches—and he'd confirmed that back in the caves. But had he actually succeeded?

I filed the information away for later.

Then I sighed, remembering my predicament. For me, there *was* no later. As far as I knew, I had no way to get in touch with Liam or the others. No way to let them know what Jonathan had just told me.

"Despite everything, Sunshine, my offer still stands," Jonathan said, gentler now. When I met his gaze again, his green eyes softened in a way that—if I'd let it—might've reminded me of all those times we'd made out in his tree fort in the woods as kids.

"Do you mean that?" I asked, pretending to consider it.

"We could be great together. You know that, Rayanne. You can feel it, just like I can." He leaned in close, slowly inching his mouth toward mine. Then, in a hoarse whisper he probably thought was sexy, "You liked the taste of my blood, didn't you? You want it again."

Doing my best to ignore the rotten stench of his breath, I smiled and let him get within a hair's breadth of my lips.

Then I spit in his face and head-butted his already smashed nose.

He howled in agony as the blood surged all over again. "You treacherous little *bitch*!"

"I tasted your blood once already, filthy hunter. That was enough."

Even after drinking all that water in the lake, the bitter tang of that blood still lingered on my lips.

Still, no matter how revolting, it would never be enough to erase the memory of Asher's fiery kiss. *That* was a kiss to remember, a taste I wanted to hold on to—at least, for as long as my memories lasted in this twisted place.

My heart squeezed. In that moment, I wished more than anything I was back in that cave with Ash. Back in his arms.

I wished we could do it all over again, without the threat of hunters and devil's traps and murdered witches. I wished we could do it just because we wanted to be together. To feel that connection. That heat.

I'd healed him—that much was obvious. But I'd never told him it was so much more than that for me.

I'm, uh… I'm pretty sure I'm falling in love with you, too. So… there's that.

I closed my eyes for just a moment, replaying his words in my mind.

"Fuck you, witch," Jonathan shouted.

I opened my eyes, unable to hold back the bubble of laughter pushing its way out.

I laughed until my sides hurt and tears streamed down my cheeks.

And then I fucking snapped.

"Newsflash, Jonathan!" I shouted. "I'm already fucked. Completely, totally, thoroughly fucked. Everyone I care about is gone—I'll never see them again. I don't even know if they're okay, or what kind of shitshow you left behind. I'm trapped in this realm for all eternity with my sworn enemy, a man—and I use that term *very* loosely—I find more repulsive than the idea of eating the demon shit I stepped in on the walk over. And now you're trying to *kiss* me? *Seriously?* You know what, Jonathan? Fuck *you*."

I hauled off and punched him in the mouth. It was an easy hit, one he hadn't seen coming, and my aim was true. But the crunch of my knuckles against his few remaining teeth was a lot less satisfying than I'd hoped.

It riled him up, though, and he came at me with renewed energy, knocking me off my feet before I could duck out of the way.

I hit the ground with a thud, then caught a sharp elbow to the face. Stars danced before my eyes and blood trickled from my nose, but I jumped back up to my feet before he could pin me down and do any more damage.

"Like it or not, Rayanne," he said, circling me again, "we stand a better chance of getting out of here if we work together."

"This is the Shadowrealm. There *is* no way out."

"There has to be. Our souls aren't trapped—we still have have our bodies."

"I don't know why we've physically manifested here, but you can't leave," I panted, swiping the back of my hand across my bloody nose. "It's over. This is your fate now. Your final destination."

"If you think this is the end, witch—"

"It is," I shouted, cutting him off before the poison of his words leeched into my thoughts. "You can chase me all over this realm. We might spend the rest of eternity beating and tormenting each other."

"That's the *least* of what I'm going to do to you."

I shook my head. "No matter what you do to me, you're never leaving here. Nothing will get you out of this. It's over."

Jonathan stared at me a long moment, his eyes boring right through me.

The realization seemed to settle over him like a shroud. In a defeated voice, he said, "If that's true, then you can't leave either."

I looked back in the direction of where I'd seen my black forest, but the landscape had shifted once again. Maybe that was how the Shadowrealm worked—different realms shifting in and out, constantly rearranging themselves.

Or maybe the forest hadn't existed at all—just a mirage fueled on hope and impossible dreams.

I swallowed the lump of regret in my throat, wondering how much longer it would be before I no longer felt that sort of thing—regret, or *any* human emotion, for that matter. Liam had warned me about this the night I'd tried to banish Travis's soul.

But… no. No matter what I'd told Jonathan, deep down I didn't regret my choice. How could I? I'd saved Ash.

Bought the others a fighting chance. That was what mattered.

"You're right," I said now. "I can't leave. That's the price I had to pay."

"Why would you *do* that?" he asked. "Why?"

I wanted to ask Jonathan if he'd ever really loved anyone, but there was no point. He may have been innocent once, but that innocence had been twisted and tarnished, leaving him incapable of love. Obsession and madness were all he knew now.

Maybe it was a tragedy. Maybe he could've turned out differently if someone had only taught him that love was boundless and beautiful.

But his father had made sure he'd never gotten that chance, and I couldn't give it to him now. Not even if I possessed all the magic in the world.

"Why?" he screamed, his voice equal parts rage and agony.

It almost—*almost*—hurt to hear him in so much pain.

I turned away from him, but not before leaving him with my answer. They were the very last words I'd likely ever speak, but I was okay with that now.

They felt like the right ones. The true ones. And for that brief moment, they brought a smile to my lips.

"To make the world a better place for the ones I left behind."

Certain he wouldn't follow me this time—and not really caring if he did, anyway—I took a step toward the spot where I'd last seen my forest. It seemed like as good a direction as any other.

But before I could take a second step, a wave of dizziness hit, followed immediately by a deep rumbling beneath my feet.

I'd felt a similar sensation one other time in my life, back when I lived in Portland, just before I'd come to Blackmoon Bay.

It was an earthquake.

The rumble quickly progressed to a tremble, then the ground shook violently. I struggled to stay upright as the forest floor cracked apart, toppling trees all around me.

I tried to run for a clearing, but the forest seemed to be thickening with new growth even as it split wide open. The landscape was changing right beneath our feet.

The ground rose up suddenly beneath me, and I skidded down the new embankment, landing on my hands and knees. With nowhere else to go, I crawled over to a large tree that hadn't moved and wrapped myself around it, holding on for dear life as the whole world fell apart.

Everywhere I looked, rock and root crumbled away into newly formed crevasses.

When the rumbling finally stopped and the dust settled, I was looking out across a great rift at least twenty feet across, stretching on in both directions for miles and miles.

I was on one side.

Jonathan on the other.

I crept to the edge and peered down inside. It was dark

and cold and bottomless, its dirt walls crawling with electric blue vines dotted with iridescent white flowers.

It was oddly beautiful.

I glanced up at Jonathan, who stood smugly on his side of the divide, arms crossed over his chest.

"There's one thing about our predicament I'm grateful for, Sunshine." He smiled, pure menace emanating like a light from inside him. "I'm over here. And you're over there. With *that*."

My stomach dropped. I could tell from the satisfaction on his face that whatever he was talking about would be bad news for me.

Swallowing hard, I turned to look over my shoulder just in time to see it: a vile, two-headed beast charging down the tree-strewn path.

Charging right for me.

EIGHT

ASHER

Two hours and countless tunnels and cells later, it was time to make an official statement: This was the most fucked-up shitshow I'd ever seen.

Gray's ex? Dude was fucking *disturbed*. It wasn't enough for him to just hunt down witches and burn them, honoring the desperate, pathetic traditions of his ancestors.

No. *This* fucking guy took things to a whole new level of sociopathy. He made Sebastian look like an angel strumming a golden harp in a meadow full of fucking tulips.

Picturing the Prince of Hell prancing around a meadow should've made me laugh, but I couldn't even crack a smile. Not here.

This place was too damn horrifying for words.

I stood in the middle of a large circular chamber in the center of the prison system, the space washed in a sickly green light that emanated from bulbs wired into the ceiling.

It smelled like shit and fear, so pungent it made my eyes itch.

The walls were lined with cages holding dozens of shifters, badly wounded and seemingly trapped in their animal forms—foxes, wolves, mountain lions, a panther. A huge copper-colored cage in the middle of the space held large birds—owls, ravens, vultures, and a bald eagle.

Perched on metal bars inside the cage, some of the birds glanced my way as I entered the room, but most of the other shifters were too weak to even lift their heads. Others cowered in the darkest corners of their cages, flinching with every step I took.

None of them uttered a sound.

"What did he do to you?" I whispered. But of course, none of them could respond.

An opening at the back of the room led to a secondary chamber about a third of the size. This one was also lined with cages, but these cages held people—humans, vampires, and a few shifters in their human form.

All of them were nude, their bodies covered in bruises and scrapes.

The vampires' cage was the largest, fitted with wooden posts inside.

All four vampires had been nailed to those posts with hawthorn stakes.

Everyone in this room was starving—and that appeared to be the least of their problems.

A pair of vampires watched silently as I approached one

of the adjacent cages. Curled up on the floor inside, two pale humans clung to each other.

They were already dead.

Bile rose in my throat. The horrors all of these creatures must've endured at the hands of that fucking psycho...

And now he's with Gray in who knows where...

I shut down that line of thinking before it could go any farther. Gray attacked *him*. She ripped out *his* soul. Wherever the hell they'd ended up after that, I had to believe Gray was on top.

Had to believe she had a plan.

Had to believe she'd come back to us.

In the meantime, I had a promise to keep.

According to the map on Shears's comm device, the cave system itself was vast, but it seemed Jonathan's crew had only used part of it. It looked like I'd already covered about two-thirds of the prison on foot, but I hadn't seen any signs of the witches. Also MIA? Fiona Brentwood, the Grinaldi vampire Gray wanted me to save.

I still had a fair bit of ground to cover, but I couldn't just leave these creatures locked up in here.

I took another look around the connected chambers and blew out a breath, trying to figure this shit out. All of them would need to be freed from this eternal hell. But how? There was no guard in sight to force into opening the cages, no sign of keys or any other tools I could use to pick the locks.

"How long have you been here?" I asked the pair of vampires—the only beings that seemed to be conscious in the back chamber. They stared vacantly ahead, unable or unwilling to respond.

"Do you know how they unlock the cages?" I tried again.

Nothing.

Moving into the main chamber, I asked if any of the shifters could shift back into human form. If I could speak to some of them, I might be able to get some information that could actually help.

But no one answered. I'd have to figure it out on my own.

I approached each cage cautiously, doing my best to scope out any potential traps or triggers. The cages appeared to be made of metal, but didn't look all that strong up close. Several of the bars were bent and rusted, others missing altogether. Most of the locks were rusty.

But now that I was scrutinizing them, I sensed something else—something that Jonathan's people probably thought was undetectable. If not for the surge of power Gray had given me, I probably *wouldn't* have noticed it.

The cages were giving off a strange, electric hum. The invisible current smelled like burning leaves. It stirred the hairs on my arms as I got close.

Slowly, I lifted my hand to the birdcage in the middle to see how close I could get. But just before I touched the metal, a harsh whisper stopped me cold.

"Asher, stop!"

I spun around at the sound of my name and caught

sight of a pale, thin woman with straight brownish hair and a dingy black dress.

Vampire.

It was Fiona, the Grinaldi traitor Darius had brought back from the east coast who'd turned out to be an old friend of Gray's from high school—a girl who'd teamed up with Jonathan to murder Sophie and hunt down Gray.

"Fiona Brentwood?" she said, as if I'd even asked for her name. "I was the one Darius—"

"I know who you are, bloodsucker. You got something to say to me? Say it fast."

She glanced over her shoulder, then scurried closer, keeping her voice at a whisper. "I know you don't have any reason to trust me, but—"

"Wait—don't tell me. I can trust you now? I should come with you if I want to live? Follow you right into a trap so your boy Jon can give you a cookie for a job well done?" I took a step closer, my muscles tensing for an attack. "Hard pass, sweetheart."

She blinked rapidly, then lowered her eyes, tears spilling down her cheeks. "He kidnapped me that night, too."

"Yeah, I'm sure you were real torn up about it."

She met my eyes again, a spark of fire flickering in hers. "I am just as much his prisoner as Gray is," she insisted. "I never—"

My hand was around her throat before I'd even registered the action. "Don't you say her fucking name to me. Don't you *ever* say it."

Despite my strength, we both knew I couldn't kill her

this way—I'd have to burn her or cut off her head—but she relented anyway, lowering her eyes and nodding in a silent promise.

I released her. I had no intention of killing her. I'd promised Gray I'd get her out of here.

"If you're his prisoner," I said, "how is it you're walking around free?"

"Jonathan went off with... with your witch," she said, careful to heed my advice and not mention Gray's name. "I think he took her out of here. Some of the guards were sent out to look for them—I heard them talking on their devices."

I didn't bother clarifying that Gray was the one who'd taken Jonathan out of here, not vice versa.

"And you managed to track me down without alerting a single guard?" I asked.

"There aren't enough guards to go around. There's too much to keep track of here, and I'm not important enough to keep track of." Sadness filled her eyes, but it flickered out quickly, replaced by an emotion I knew well.

I'd once spent a lot of time nurturing it. Feeding it. And now that same intensity rolled off her body in waves.

Vengeance.

I blew out a breath, not sure how to play this. A woman scorned could go either way, throwing her man under the bus one minute, jumping into his arms the next.

Partnering up was a risky proposition. But letting her walk? Not happening. Fiona was a loose end I couldn't afford to leave untied, and she'd spent more time in this place—and in Jonathan's presence—than I had. Maybe she *could* help me.

"Let's get something clear, Fangs." I grabbed her face, forcing her to meet my eyes. "The only reason you're not a pile of ashes right now is that Gray thought you deserved a second chance."

The vengeance in her eyes melted into another emotion I knew well: regret.

"But I don't," she whispered.

"Maybe not. But Gray seemed to think there was still some good left in you." I released her and fished out one of the comm devices, handing it over. "Here's the deal. I'm giving you that second chance you don't deserve. And you're going to earn it back retroactively."

She took the device as if it was the most precious gift anyone had ever given her. "Thank... Thank you."

"Don't thank me yet, Fangs. You've got a lot of hard work ahead of you."

She wiped the tears from her face and nodded quickly. "Where do we start?"

I jerked my head toward the cages behind us. "What do you know about the cages?"

"You can't touch the bars. They're all fae spelled—everything here is."

Fae spelled? That would explain the high-tech gear and why I was pretty sure none of the guys could sense our presence here.

So the little fucker *was* working with the fae.

"Does the name Orendiel ring any bells?" I asked Fiona.

Her eyes widened. "How do you know Orendiel?"

"I'm more interested in how *you* know him."

"I don't. Not personally," she said quickly, but there was a note of reverence in her voice that hadn't been there a second ago. "He's one of the fae helping Jonathan."

"Helping how, exactly?"

"I don't know all the details—Jonathan cut me out of his plans a while ago. He'd already been working with other supers before that. You know, disgruntled mercenary types. But the fae thing is new."

"Care to speculate on their arrangement?"

"From what I could piece together, Orendiel heard about Jonathan's work and approached him about partnering up. I think Orendiel made him some kind of deal—fae weapons and tech in exchange for a place on Jonathan's team."

That was a disturbing thought. One lone psycho could easily influence a contingent of aging hunters like Shears and Smokey Joe. But fae were notorious tricksters, and they weren't easily swayed. If Orendiel had truly wanted a spot on the team—enough to approach Jonathan like that—then Jonathan must've been working on something major. Something that went far beyond kidnapping witches and torturing supernaturals.

Like weaponized devil's traps, you idiot.

A chill ran down my spine as the pieces clicked into place. For all Jonathan's mad scientist craziness, he'd already made some pretty disastrous discoveries. Discoveries that could bring the supernatural world to its knees.

And now the fae had their hands in it.

"We need to get everyone out of here," I said. "And then I need to find the witches."

Fiona sighed. "Even if we could figure out how to open the cages, what then?" Her shoulders sagged. "Look at them, Asher. They've been starved, beaten, tormented. Nobody in this room is walking out on their own two feet. Or four feet. Or wings, for that matter."

Much as I hated to admit it, Fangs had a point.

"We need to heal them," she went on, surveying the poor beasts. "At least, the ones who are still alive. If we can get their strength up, some of them might stand a chance."

"Great. I don't suppose you have a stash of psycho hunter antivenin on you?"

"No, but..." She tapped her lips, her brow furrowed in concentration. After a beat, her eyes lit up, and a slow smile spread across her lips. "I've got the next best thing." Fiona pushed up her sleeve. "Vampire blood."

"I'm listening."

"There are four other vampires here. Once we stop the hawthorn poisoning, their bodies should start to regenerate. I can help speed up the process with some of my blood. Once they're strong enough, they can help me with the others."

"Vampire blood won't work on shifters."

"It might on *these* shifters." She glanced around at the caged beasts, then sighed. "They're hybrids."

"So, shifter and...?"

"Vampire."

My eyes widened. I didn't even want to *know* how Jonathan had pulled off that fucked-up feat.

"Alright," I said. "First things first. How do we get past the fae mojo?"

"That's the thing—we can't." Her shoulders sagged again. "Not without the keycards."

I shoved a hand through my hair, damn near ready to tear it out. "So we're right back at square—Wait a minute. Keycards?"

She nodded. "The lead guards carry them. They look like—"

"This?" I pulled out the wallet I'd jacked from Smokey Joe and flashed the collection of black cards.

"Where did you get that?" she asked, but she was already reaching for my arm, tugging me toward the main chamber's entrance. "Check the walls. There should be a panel."

"I don't see anything."

"It's spelled to look like the rock. You have to feel for it. It's not as cool as the real rock around it."

We each took a side and methodically worked our way across the walls. She found the panel a few minutes later, opening it to reveal a series of card readers and red LCD lights.

After a good bit of trial and error, we managed to find the right cards, swipe, and turn all the red lights green.

The electric hum vanished.

Locks clicked all around us, and a couple of the cages swung open.

Still, none of the creatures moved. Fiona certainly had her work cut out for her.

"Do you know where he's keeping the witches?" I asked, tucking the keycards back into my pocket. "I'll free them, then we'll reconvene here and figure out how to get everyone the fuck out of this place."

Fiona nodded. "They're all on C-block."

I pulled up the map on her comms device, hoping like hell my trust hadn't been misplaced. "Show me."

NINE

GRAY

That monster could *move*.

While Jonathan watched on impassively from the other side of the rift, I bolted into the forest, dodging between felled trees and hopping over crevices, trying to outrun the beast chasing me.

It was the size of an SUV with the body shape of a lion, two dragon-like heads, and a spiked tail that looked like it could do some serious damage to my skull. The only thing saving me was the fact that it was too big to fit between some of the trees, so it couldn't always keep up with me. But no matter how hard I ran, the thing showed no signs of tiring, always waiting for me on the other side.

With nowhere else to hide, I circled back toward the lake, hoping like hell the beast couldn't swim.

I dove straight in and swam for the center. When I got to what I assumed was the deepest part, I bobbed up out of the water and whipped around to look for signs of my would-be attacker.

He paced the shoreline, as if he were trying to decide on the best way in. Razor-sharp claws glinted on all four of his giant paws, leaving deep holes in the muddy embankment wherever he stepped.

Please don't swim… please don't swim…

Still watching me, he stopped pacing and reared up on his hind legs, letting loose a violent roar that left ripples in the lake and reverberated through my chest.

When the awful sound finally stopped, he crashed back down onto his front paws.

And—*poof!*—the entire lake evaporated.

Without warning, I fell a good twenty feet, landing on my ass on the lake's muddy bottom.

It knocked the wind out of me, but that fall… it should've killed me. At the very least, it should've broken most of the bones in my body.

Instead, it just made everything hurt.

I scrambled to my feet, struggling against the slippery mud. Pain echoed through my bones.

Now I was *completely* screwed. I was twenty feet deep in a pit with walls made out of mud, and the animal was already making his way toward me with ease.

As soon as he reached the bottom of the former lake, he charged at me once again, faster than lightning.

I had no time to react. He was on me in a heartbeat, knocking me flat on my back, pinning me down as each one of his demonic heads sank their sharp, filthy teeth into my shoulders, piercing my flesh down to the bone.

A shock of the most terrible pain I'd ever felt shot through my body, burning an agonizing path from my shoulders to my fingers, then down my back.

I couldn't scream. I couldn't cry. I couldn't even breathe.

I wanted to curl into a ball and die. As long as the burning stopped, I didn't care.

But deep inside me, a glimmer of my magic sparked to life, temporarily breaking through the haze of pain.

Fight, Gray. Fight!

I seized on it, coaxing the magic to life with sheer will. My palms warmed as the magic gathered strength, and once again I drew power from the earth, feeling it soak into me everywhere my body touched the muddy ground.

Ignoring the pain in my arms, I slammed my palms into the beast's heads, unleashing all of that power.

Bright blue light exploded around us.

The beast recoiled, skittering off of me and hissing in pain, his heads trapped in twin bubbles of light. He tried to shake free, but the harder he fought, the more the magic seemed to disorient him.

I crawled over to the edge and climbed up the embankment, slipping with every step, but desperate to get away before the magic wore off. My arms were throbbing again, but I couldn't stop. Couldn't look back.

I was struggling to reach the top when a black-gloved hand thrust out above my head, offering help.

I took it without thinking, allowing the stranger to haul

me up. My shoulders burned with the effort of holding on, but I gritted my teeth and scrambled up the last part of the muddy embankment, grateful for the rescue just the same.

He gave one last tug, and I was out. I landed on my back on the grass, trembling and spent. For several heart-beats, I stared up at the sky, now violet with orange sherbet clouds, and tried to catch my breath.

"Thank you," I finally managed.

A hooded figure loomed over me, all darkness and shadow…

Except for those otherworldly electric blue eyes.

TEN

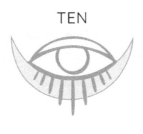

GRAY

"Liam!" His name caught in my throat, emotion choking off my words. Ignoring the pain in my body, I got to my feet and wrapped my arms around his neck, burying my face in his shadowy black robes.

He was back in his Death form, but I didn't care. I had never been so happy to see him.

"I didn't think I'd ever see you again. I thought..." I couldn't get the words out. My heart was hammering, filled with a strange mixture of shock and relief and joy.

After what felt like an eternity, I released my hold on him and took a step back, looking up into those luminous eyes. The realm had shifted again—or we were somehow in a new place—the lake vanishing and the forest turning into a meadow carpeted in blue and silver grass. It seemed like Jonathan and the two-headed beast were gone, but I didn't dare break my gaze away from Liam to find out.

How long had it been since I'd last seen him—since that

brief glimpse in my realm before Jonathan hauled me back into the caves? Weeks? A month?

"How did you find me?" I asked.

Liam was stone-still. He hadn't said a word.

And, I realized now, he hadn't hugged me back. Hadn't shown a single sign that he was happy or relieved to see me.

"Liam?" I whispered, my heart hammering for an entirely different reason now. Had something happened to the guys? To Haley and Reva and the others? "What... what happened?"

A frosty breeze kissed my face, my breath turning into white fog.

"What have you done, Shadowborn?" Liam asked plainly. His voice was dead calm; more than the sudden chill in the air, that utter lack of emotion sent a shiver down my spine.

All traces of Liam—of his humanity—were gone, and when he reached up and wrapped his hands around my upper arms, my blood turned icy cold.

"*What*," he repeated, "have you done?"

He was talking about Jonathan's soul, I realized. About how I'd condemned myself to this fate, even after all the warnings he'd given me the night I'd tried to banish Travis.

"I had to do *something*!" I said. "I couldn't just let him torture and kill—"

"And banishing yourself to an eternity here was the best option you could come up with? All your magic, all your training, all your instincts... and *this*?" He glanced out across the realm. "*This* is the path you choose?"

"You think I *wanted* this?" I jerked free of his grasp, anger turning my blood from cold to hot once again. "I was a prisoner, Liam. In every sense of the word. So I saw an opening and I took it."

"It was reckless. Foolish. It was—"

"The only way I could get Jonathan out of that prison and save my friends."

His eyes blazed, his icy, stoic demeanor finally shattering. I hated fighting with him, but I'd take that over the nothingness any day of the week.

"And now he is here, trapped as you are trapped. You have banished him, but not destroyed him. As long as you are both here, he will hunt you. Eternally. And each time you're caught, you will be forced to relive his cruel torments. Endlessly."

"And each time *he's* caught, he will relive mine."

Liam was impassive once again.

"I made him, Liam," I went on, the words leaving a path of fire in my throat, burning as only the most difficult truths could. "Just as he made me. This was the only way."

Jonathan and I had been in love once. Then, he'd tried to kill me. He spent the rest of his life hunting me down, dreaming of my death, dreaming of stealing my power. That more than anything was his life's work, his ultimate quest. It shaped the boy he used to be into the man he ultimately became.

And me? I spent the rest of my life fearing the day he'd

come for me. The day he'd hurt more people that I love. The day he'd make good on that age-old promise.

When I find you, I will burn you.

If we'd never crossed paths as teenagers, how different would our lives have become?

"I couldn't leave him there to wreak havoc on my friends," I said. "On anyone. They don't deserve that."

Liam's eyes softened just a fraction. "You no more made him than I made this place. He *exists*, Gray. He made choices, just as you made choices."

"Choices you obviously don't agree with."

"Gray..." Liam sighed and turned his back on me, igniting a flicker of shame in my chest. Was he that disappointed and angry that he couldn't even look me in the eye?

"You are never leaving this place," he continued. "All of those friends you were so desperate to help? They will have to find a way to go on without you now. You have no future. No fate. No destiny. Only this." He swept an arm out before him, indicating the vast, endless hills, now glittering beneath the light of two moons. It was eerily beautiful, like the vines and flowers I'd seen in the crevasse.

There were no monsters in sight.

"Is it really so terrible?" I took a step closer to him, but a sharp bite of pain in my foot stopped me.

I lifted it to take a look. Blood soaked through the fabric I'd wrapped around it.

"Not at all terrible," Liam said sarcastically, finally turning to face me again. "Especially if you enjoy long walks in the moonlight through meadows of razor-sharp grass."

My eyes widened. I tried not to move.

"Nothing is what it seems here, Gray. You can't trust anything or anyone you encounter."

Yeah, I was starting to figure that out.

"Why does it keep changing?" I asked. "What happened to the lake pit? Before that, I was trapped in some kind of volcanic wasteland for weeks." I told him about the fire demons, the smoke, how the lake initially healed my wounds.

"The Shadowrealm comprises many different worlds. No, not all of them are terrible. Some are quite peaceful, even restorative. An unburdened soul could travel to her final destination rather pleasantly, lingering in beautiful places as she pleased, healing the spiritual wounds she'd endured in life. Others, however, encounter all manner of demons, monsters, fears, nightmares, regrets—not to mention the physical challenges of landscapes like this. If they fail those challenges, if they refuse to fight those battles, if they give up without trying, if they allow the realm to destroy the last spark of their humanity, they end up in what your kind refers to as hell, though that is really just another realm, like so many in our universe."

A stone bridge appeared before us, and the sharp grass beneath it dropped away, revealing a dark blue river dotted with lotus blossoms. Liam gestured for me to step onto the bridge, and he followed close behind.

When I turned to look at him again, he was back in his

human form, dressed in jeans and a soft-looking flannel, his blond hair flopping into his eyes. My heart kicked up a notch at the sight, but the rest of my body relaxed. He was much easier to talk to as Liam.

"Hi," I said, my voice strangely shy.

"Hello." Liam chuckled softly, and my stomach did a little flip.

Had his laugh always sounded so warm? So comforting? I wanted to hear it again, but the moment passed.

He looked away and continued along the bridge ahead of me.

Overheard, two moons merged into one, its light glimmering on the calm river beneath the bridge. Crickets sang in the distance, and a warm, gentle breeze stirred the trees that had cropped up around us.

The cut on my foot seemed to have healed, and I realized my shoulders no longer ached.

"My wounds are gone," I said.

"Yes, the realm has given you a gift. Be grateful, but wary."

We continued to the center of the bridge, then stopped to watch the river drift past below, the lotus blooms floating like little boats. The air was thick with the scent of jasmine and fresh mud.

"Sophie…" I began, but couldn't bring myself to ask the question.

Liam seemed to understand anyway. "Sophie passed through this realm as she was intended to do."

"I thought I saw her."

"Yes. She's always with you." He pressed his hand to my heart, and my skin warmed at his touch. "Here."

"Did she have to fight those... things? The fire demons? Or that two-headed beast?"

"No." Liam laced his fingers through mine and gently urged me across the rest of the stone bridge. The human warmth of his touch sent little sparks skittering up my arm, making me feel fizzy.

I wondered if he felt it too.

The river faded from sight as we walked, and by the time we reached the other side, it had vanished completely, replaced with large, flat-topped boulders. There were no trees now, just a field of big rocks.

At least they didn't look sharp or on fire.

We started making our way across the boulder field, the moon still bright overhead, illuminating our steps.

"Where are we going?" I asked as Liam helped me scramble up one of the larger boulders.

"I don't know. The realm will reveal that as you travel. I cannot influence or alter that for you, nor can I bring you home."

I nodded. I'd known that going into this. Right now, I was just grateful for his company.

"How will I know what my path is if everything keeps changing?" I asked.

It was a few moments before Liam spoke again, and when he did, his voice was heavy with regret. "You broke the natural order and came here outside the confines of your natural death. As such, while you may see glimpses of your intended path, it no longer exists as an unbroken route. You are a wanderer here, Gray. You will continue to face demons both within and without, and you will experience joys beyond your comprehension, only to have them cruelly snatched away. You will be chased and tormented and tested beyond your limits. You will be healed, only to face the same cruel brutality once again. And in the end, it will lead you nowhere."

I nodded again, swallowing the lump in my throat. It was done. There was no point crying over it, no point looking for loopholes. In this horrible in-between, I could bruise, I could break, and I could suffer. But I could never be killed.

So whatever this place had in store for me, I had to face it. That was the deal I'd signed up for when I hijacked Jonathan's soul.

"And Jonathan?" I asked.

"He is in a similar predicament. I suspect your paths will cross often. I suspect..." Liam trailed off, his face crumpling. When he met my eyes, his own were haunted, as though my current predicament was his decision. His punishment for me. "I'm so sorry, Gray."

I reached up and swept the fall of hair from his eyes, sliding my hand down to his chest. His human heart beat strong and steady, and I pressed my palm against it, trying to memorize the rhythm. "It's not your fault. I made this choice. I knew the consequences. You didn't—"

"And therein lies the problem, Gray Desario. I *didn't*." He grabbed my hand, bringing it to his lips and pressing a kiss to my fingers, a quick but surprisingly passionate gesture that totally took me off guard. "There was so much more I could've shown you, explained to you, guided you through, but I didn't. I've existed as long as the very spark of life itself, yet for this one task, I simply… ran out of time."

"It's not your fault," I repeated, but Liam seemed to be beating himself up pretty hard. Squeezing his hand, I said, "I'm just glad you're here now. How did you even find me?"

"Your magic signature. I've been trying to locate you ever since Darius told me you'd been taken, but this is the first I've sensed your power. Other than your all-too-brief appearance in your realm when you told me you'd been taken to Raven's Cape, there has been no sign of you until now."

My eyes widened. I wasn't sure he'd even gotten my message—Jonathan had yanked me back out of my realm almost as soon as I'd arrived, and I hadn't been able to return.

"Did you tell the guys about Raven's Cape?" I asked hopefully. "Did they get Asher? Is everyone okay?"

"Unfortunately, I have not been in touch with anyone since I learned of your disappearance." Liam lowered his eyes. "There hasn't been time, Gray. On the material plane, only a few hours have passed since I saw you in your realm."

"But… What?" My mind spun, trying to make sense of

his words. I was terrified to ask the next question, but I had to know. "How... How long have I been gone?"

"In linear time, you were taken by Jonathan approximately two days ago."

A strangled gasp was all I could manage. *Two days?* How was that possible when I'd already been wandering *this* place for... God, it'd felt like weeks.

"Time moves differently here, Gray," Liam explained. "That is yet another challenge you must face. You may experience the progression of seasons in a single afternoon. Your body may age thirty years in a heartbeat. Then again, you may age backward until you are a toddler, only to relive the entire experience forward again."

I nodded slowly, the full impact of what I'd done finally starting to settle in.

"Is it always like that for you?" I asked. "Traveling back and forth? How do you keep the time straight?"

"Generally, I don't. I hadn't a need for it. Not until you came into my awareness." He smiled softly, cupping my face with his hand. Despite his smile, sadness lingered in his eyes. "Understand, Gray—my life, for lack of a better phrase, is not meant to move linearly. It is only humans who experience time as a straight line of befores, durings, and afters, and that's not even real. Humans disassociated from their natural ability to perceive alternate realities and created the construct of time to bring order to a natural chaos they found too frightening to accept."

"But what about when you're in a human vessel? Aren't you limited by Liam's human perceptions?"

"Yes, that does… complicate things."

I thought about how many times he'd traveled back and forth to the material plane, constantly changing forms from his natural state to his human vessel. About how many times he'd endured that confusion and complication… just for me.

"You can stay in your Death form," I said. "I don't mind."

"Perhaps not." Liam frowned, brushing a tangled curl behind my ear. "But you don't look at me the same way."

"I… I never meant to disappoint you," I said.

"Oh, Gray. You haven't disappointed me." He stroked my cheek with his thumb. "You couldn't."

"Then why are you looking at me like that?" I whispered, lowering my eyes. I couldn't handle the intensity in his gaze. The scrutiny. He could see my soul, my heart, and he was making me feel things I didn't want to feel right now. Not while I was trapped here, facing down an eternity alone.

"There's no coming back from this, Gray," he said gently. "You risked everything. You… you *sacrificed…* everything."

"So you keep reminding me."

"I just meant…" He slid a finger under my chin and tipped my face up, forcing me to meet his eyes again. "It takes courage and selflessness to do what you've done. You must never forget that."

My heart swelled at his kindness. He was so real in that moment—a touch of compassion in an otherwise deathly place. His warmth, his eyes, the shy smile playing on his lips… Looking at him reminded me what it felt like to miss something. To miss someone.

"Will you find the others?" I asked. "And tell them about the prison? Asher is working on getting Haley and the others out." I told him about the things we'd endured there, and the parts of Jonathan's crazy plans we were able to put together from his ranting monologues.

"I will go to them, and I will tell them everything," he said when I finished. "But I don't understand—how was the incubus able to overcome the blood-born devil's trap? Surely you didn't remove his soul again?"

My cheeks flamed at the memory. "I… he was… healed. Sort of magically. Energetically."

"Magically energetically?"

"We didn't have much time," I said.

"But incubuses require—" Liam cut off suddenly, clearing his throat. "Ah. I see. I'm, um, well, it's good that you were there to… He's very lucky to have a friend… Okay." He cleared his throat again, then glanced up, taking a breath of night air. Clouds were moving in now, darkening the lavender sky to a deep slate.

"It's going to rain," he said, a hint of alarm tingeing his voice. "You need to take shelter. There's a cave system ahead—hopefully, it will still be there when we reach it."

"And if it isn't?"

Liam glanced up at the clouds. "Then I'm afraid we're in serious trouble."

ELEVEN

GRAY

The rain began as a gentle mist that floated down from the sky, descending on us like a gossamer curtain.

"Take this," Liam said, and I turned to find him unbuttoning his flannel. He shucked out of it and handed it over. "Put it over your head, and don't look up at the rain. Try your best not to take deep breaths."

"What are you talking about? It's just—"

"Take it, Gray. Do it now."

I reached for the shirt, trying not to ogle his bare chest, his well-defined arms, the way his abs bunched as he leaned closer. There was a small tattoo peeking out over his hip bone that looked a bit like a... a pineapple, maybe? Before I could confirm, he motioned again for me to cover up, and I indulged him, draping the flannel over my head and letting the sleeves hang down over my shoulders.

His scent was all around me, a mixture of ocean and sunshine and a deep, ancient earthiness that called to something just as ancient inside me. My magic responded, too, unleashing a curl of heat low in my belly.

Or maybe that wasn't my magic at all. Maybe it was just my body's response to someone who was starting to feel less like a strange, otherworldly being and more like a friend. More like a man.

We picked up the pace, Liam taking the lead, but the rain picked up, too. It was pleasant at first, cool and refreshing, but it quickly turned sharp and icy, stinging me even through the flannel.

Suddenly my chest felt tight, and I coughed hard into my hand. My fingers came away splattered with blood.

"Blood," Liam said without turning around. "We've wandered into one of the least hospitable worlds of the Shadowrealm. When it's not raining acid, it's raining glass. You're breathing it in right now. It's attacking your lung tissue."

"But it's barely sprinkling!"

"Imagine what a downpour will do. Keep moving. Don't look up."

We walked on for another five minutes, the rain gathering strength, scraping my shoulders and the tops of my feet. Blood ran in rivulets down Liam's bare back, but he refused to take his shirt back.

"Just keep moving," he said. "I see the cave ahead. Quickly!"

No sooner had we cleared the boulder field and entered the mouth of the cave did the downpour begin in earnest. From the safety of our shelter, I watched open-mouthed as thousands of glass needles pelted the ground we'd just vacated, shattering into powder on impact.

It sounded like the tinkling of tiny bells.

It was terrifyingly beautiful.

Another cough rattled through my lungs, tearing up my throat on the way out.

"That will pass, as long as you don't go back out in the rain." Liam put a hand on my shoulder, gently guiding me away from the mouth and into a large chamber deeper inside. It was close enough to the cave entrance that it still held a bit of light—just enough to make out Liam's silhouette. It was warmer than I expected, and the air smelled homey rather than dank.

When he crouched down to light a fire, I realized why.

This cave was someone's home—or it had been. There was a fire pit in the center, now glowing brightly, and several animal-skin rugs arranged around it.

"It's not a five-star resort," Liam said, rising up to his feet and dusting off his hands. "But you'll be safe in here until I get back."

"Luckily I'm not a five-star resort kind of girl." I smiled, handing back his shirt. "Besides, it's kind of cozy. Plenty of room for a sectional and a flat screen, if you're ever in the mood to redecorate."

"I'll keep it in mind." Liam laughed. The firelight caught in his eyes, and I wanted him to stay, more than anything. To keep laughing like that. To keep looking at me like that.

But after a beat, his smile faded. He reached for my

hands, his thumbs brushing gently across my knuckles. The same sparks I'd felt before skittered across my skin.

"Is there anything else you need for the night?" he asked, his voice low and husky. God, if this had been any other situation, I might've thought he wanted to... to kiss me. But that was impossible. He was Death. Death didn't just go around kissing people. Did he?

"Gray?"

"No! I mean, I... I don't suppose you have any food?" I asked hopefully.

Liam shook his head. "Your body doesn't actually need food here. Or water. Your brain is still adjusting to that reality, but once it does, you won't feel hungry or tired anymore."

Disappointment settled into that gaping hole in my stomach where the food should've been. I *liked* feeling hungry and tired. Hungry and tired were temporary problems. *Human* problems.

If my brain stopped feeling those things, what was next? How long before I lost all traces of my humanity.

Sensing my distress, Liam frowned and cupped my face, his touch warm and gentle. In that same low, husky voice, he said, "I will do what I can to protect you here, Gray."

I nodded, grateful. "But is that... allowed?"

Liam considered me for a long moment. At least, it *felt* like a long moment, standing in the spotlight of his intense gaze, holding my breath in anticipation of all the reasons why he couldn't interfere with the natural order, how I'd already caused enough trouble, how he'd already broken all the rules.

His thumb brushed across my cheek. When he finally answered, his voice was no more than a whisper.

"No," he said simply. "It isn't."

I was trapped in his eyes, losing myself in their depths, in the gentle touch of his hand on my cheek. The fire crackled behind us, soft orange light dancing with the shadows on the cave walls, the tinkling glass rain falling outside. In that moment, it seemed like we'd hit the pause button on all the craziness of the situation, and in here, it was just us, warm and close and safe.

If I stretch up on my tiptoes just a little bit, our lips will touch...

"Gray, I..." Liam let out a soft sigh, his gaze sweeping down to my lips. He seemed to be stuck there, maybe contemplating the same thing I was contemplating.

Holy hell, he's going to kiss me...

"Liam, I—"

"I should go," he said quickly, our words crashing into each other. "I, ah, I'm sorry, Gray. I hate to leave you alone here, but I need to get back to the material plane and find your people."

I nodded, turning away from him and pretending to be interested in the fire. What the hell just happened? Had I actually been thinking about kissing Liam? Not just thinking about it, but... *wanting* it?

"No, you're right," I said, forcing conviction into my words. "You need to tell the guys everything I've told you about Jonathan and the prison. It's crucial that they help Ash and the others."

"Yes," he said. "But what shall I tell them of you?"

"Tell them…" I closed my eyes, trying to picture each of their faces, trying to find the words to say goodbye. What could I say? That I loved them? That I appreciated everything they'd done for me? That I wished we'd had more time to get to know each other, to be together, to be a family?

That I was sorry?

Fuck that.

A surge of anger welled up inside, pushing outward against my skin as if it were a living thing trying to break out. Jonathan and his family had taken so much from me as a child, and now I was in the same predicament again, still trying to outrun him. Separated once again from the people I most cared about. Alone and powerless…

But… *no*. That was bullshit. I wasn't an orphaned, powerless child on the run and afraid of my own magic anymore. I was a *witch*. Maybe I didn't have full control of it yet, but everything inside me believed—no, *knew*—that I had power.

My anger burned away, leaving something much stronger in its wake: raw determination.

I turned back toward Liam. "You tell them I'll be home as soon as I can."

"Gray, I don't think it's wise to make that sort of statement when—"

"You told me if I banished a soul here against its will,

my own soul would be trapped here eternally while my body rotted away on the material plane. But my body *isn't* on earth. It's here. And so is my magic."

"That may be true, but you can't just magic your way out of the Shadowrealm. That's not how it works."

"The fact that I manifested here proves we don't actually *know* how it works." I shook my head, dislodging a thought that had been quietly needling me ever since I'd seen the black forest by that lake, right before Jonathan attacked me. "Every time I've traveled to my own magic realm, I've encountered the black forest and the rune gate—the borderlands between my realm and the Shadowrealm. The gate was always leading me here."

"But not for the purpose which ultimately vanquished you here." Liam ran a hand through his hair, exasperated. "Gray, you were supposed to train as a Shadowborn, to learn how to harness magic from both realms and work with soul energy, both light and dark, in whichever capacity we ultimately determined best suited you. Instead, you condemned a soul here before his natural death, and now—"

"I know what I did, but that's not the point. All I'm saying is a connection between realms doesn't just break. I *saw* the black forest here—it vanished before I could get to it, but it was still here. Which means my realm is still accessible."

"The Shadowrealm is endless and ever-shifting. You can't possibly know if and when the forest will appear, or if your rune gate will even be in the same place. I understand your desire to find the loophole in this, Gray. I just don't want you to—"

"To what, Liam? Hope? Well too bad. I *am* hoping. Hope is the most human thing about me right now, and I'm not giving it up, no matter how tough the odds are, no matter how crazy I sound. Hope is my life raft, and you can bet your ancient, all-powerful ass I'm clinging to that bitch until my very last breath. If the black forest doesn't reappear, I'm just going to have to find another way to the rune gate. If that rune gate is a pile of rubble, I'm just going to have to make another one. So you go back to the material plane and you tell Emilio to have a hot batch of brownies ready for me, because as soon as I find the way out of this nightmare, I'm coming home."

With no room for argument and nothing left to say, Liam nodded brusquely, then vanished, leaving his signature black feather floating in the air between us.

He was gone before I could be sure, but I swore I caught the hint of a smile on his lips.

TWELVE

RONAN

"I smell a bloodsucker on the porch." Elena handed me the last plate to dry and turned off the faucet, reaching for the towel on her shoulder. "Tell me he belongs to you or I'll go out and behead him."

"Beaumont?" Hell, it was still daylight. What was he doing here? I bolted for the front door and wrenched it open, the sight nearly knocking me on my ass.

Liam stood on the front porch in human form, looking like some kind of half-stoned, post-Grunge Ken doll. Darius was leaning against him, his arm draped over Liam's shoulder, his feet barely touching the ground.

I couldn't even tell if he was conscious.

I opened the door and gestured them inside just as Elena stepped into the foyer, still holding the towel.

"*Madre María!*" Elena gasped when she saw Liam, stumbling backward against the wall and pressing the towel to her heart. "You're…"

"Not here for you," Liam assured her. Then, to me, "It seems I've found your vampire."

"I'm no one's vampire," Darius slurred. "I am a king. The king of blood and bones. Bones are... important."

"Get him on the couch," I said. "Elena, close all the blinds."

I shouted for Emilio, who'd been in the back bedroom checking in with the Blackmoon Bay PD.

Liam laid Darius on the couch in the living room. The vampire was babbling and delirious, the skin on his hands and face black and blistering where it'd been scorched by the sun. He was wearing a black hoodie I'd left at the motel, but from the looks of things, it hadn't offered much coverage.

"Did you find him like this?" I asked Liam.

"Yes. I sensed his dire situation the moment I materialized here, and located him in a garden shed about four miles away. I don't know how long he'd been exposed to the sun before that. I brought him here posthaste."

"What's going on?" Emilio emerged from the hall, his face falling as he took in the scene. "Shit! What happened? Why isn't he at the motel?"

"He hasn't said a coherent word yet," Liam said.

Emilio propped Darius's head up with a pillow, wincing at the sight of his face. Angry black patches covered his cheeks and nose, the skin charred and cracked. His lips were a blistered mess. His chin and neck were stained a rusty brown that could only be one thing.

"Blood," I said, wiping at it with my thumb.

"It's…" Darius began to shiver uncontrollably, his teeth chattering, his fangs protruding and retracting on their own.

He needed to heal. He needed nourishment. Now.

Without a second thought, I pushed up my sleeve and pressed my wrist to his mouth. Fresh or not, demon blood was never a vamp's first choice, but it would have to do.

Darius clamped his mouth shut and turned his head away from the offering.

"Don't be a dick," I said. "Just hold your non-existent breath and pretend it's one of those snooty French wines you love so much."

I pressed harder, but he shoved my arm away—a gesture that took a hell of a lot of effort for a vampire with supposed superhuman strength.

"Can't," he said, his voice cracking. "Too… much."

"Too much what?" Emilio knelt down next to me in front of the couch, his eyes full of concern.

I unzipped the sweatshirt. The once stark-white dress shirt underneath was soaked in blood.

"There's our answer," I said.

Shit. He'd fed on someone. Maybe even multiple some-ones. And it hadn't been a clean job, either, which meant it wasn't consensual.

That was bad news.

I shot Emilio a worried look. Before all hell broke loose with Gray last month, Darius and I hadn't exactly been close—not for a long time. But I was pretty damn sure forced feedings weren't his style. He had too much honor and dignity for that.

"Who was it?" I tried to ask Darius. "And why were you out in the sun?"

He tried to sit up, his eyes blazing as he grabbed my wrist. "Attacked by—" he began, but his words died, his eyelids drooping closed.

He'd finally passed out.

It was probably for the best. His body needed to shut down everything else so it could focus on healing. For bloodsuckers, sun poisoning wasn't like knife wounds or broken bones. The effects of it could linger for days, and it required a lot more effort to undo the damage. The blood was a double-edged sword, too; he'd obviously fed recently, and fresh blood would help him heal faster. But too much of it would wreak havoc on his nervous system first.

"He OD'd," I told Emilio, pure and simple.

"OD'd? But Darius doesn't feed on—"

"I don't know what to tell you, Alvarez. He's covered in human blood and he's completely fucked up."

Emilio took one more look at Darius, then nodded.

Leaving the vampire to rest, Emilio and I joined Elena in the kitchen, where she was scraping what looked like chopped weeds from her cutting board into a mug. The teakettle whistled on the stove.

"How's your friend?" she asked, turning off the flame and returning to her chopping.

"Too soon to tell," Emilio said.

Elena nodded, but thankfully didn't press. "And the other... guy?"

"Liam," Emilio said.

"Friend of yours?"

"It's... complicated." This from the man in question, who'd slipped into the kitchen like a damn ghost. I almost preferred his Death form—it was creepy as fuck, but at least with the black robes and mysterious riddle-speak, I knew what I was getting. I didn't think I'd ever get used to seeing him as a regular guy, no matter how artfully messed his surfer-blond hair was, or how much fucking flannel he wore.

"I am bound to a witch in their company," he continued. "She's Sh—"

"She's the one missing," I said to Elena, then shot Liam a warning glare. As far as Emilio and I were concerned, that was all Elena needed to know about Gray.

Liam wisely shut his trap.

Emilio leaned in close to Elena, lowering his voice. "You, ah, may want to send someone over to Seaside Motel to check things out. Darius obviously fed on someone, and he mentioned some kind of attack."

Elena slammed her knife down on the cutting board and gave Emilio a look that could've turned Hawaii into a frozen wasteland, but she slid the phone from her back pocket and made the call anyway.

"Yeah, it's Alvarez," she said into the phone. "Send a car over to Seaside Motel. Make sure he's one of us—I don't want any humans in on this, just in case there's—" She paused, then sighed. "Are you serious? Alright, cancel that car. Just keep me posted if anything else turns up."

She disconnected and looked at Emilio. "Room fourteen?"

Emilio nodded.

"Apparently a housekeeper reported a domestic disturbance a couple of hours ago, but when one of ours arrived on the scene, she told him she'd been mistaken—it was just the television. My officer asked around, but no one else heard anything. When he entered the room, everything seemed in order. The television was blaring, but that was it. No one was around."

I looked to Emilio. "If something happened at the motel, Darius must've called his clean-up crew."

"Vampire influence," he said, shaking his head. "Hell of a drug."

"In this case," Elena snapped, resuming her angry weed-chopping, "a hell of a lucky break for you two. You come back here after twenty years, and this is what you bring to my doorstep?"

"He was supposed to wait for us at the motel until sundown," Emilio explained. "I don't know what happened."

"Maybe he decided to order in some room service," she said.

I shook my head. "That's not Darius's style."

"He's a vampire, Ronan. It's exactly his style."

"No, it isn't." Emilio folded his arms over his massive

chest and leaned back against the counter, his jaw tight. "He doesn't feed on live humans."

Emilio was right. I was pretty sure the only time Beaumont had even *tasted* human blood recently was the night he and Gray made their pact and he sealed the blood bond. Now he was overdosing?

Elena picked up the kettle and poured steaming water into the mug full of weeds, then covered it with a saucer. "It needs to steep for a couple of hours."

"What is it?"

"A tincture—just a few herbs from the garden. It should help neutralize the effect of the blood, allowing his body to focus on healing from the sun poisoning."

Emilio raised an eyebrow.

"Shifters and vampires aren't always good bedfellows," she explained, "but here in the RC, the freaks stick together."

"Better watch yourself, Elena," he teased. "Someone might start thinking you actually *care*."

For the first time since we woke up in her house this morning, Elena actually laughed. It changed her entire face.

Emilio's, too.

THIRTEEN

RONAN

"I was attacked," Darius explained, sipping Elena's concoction. He'd yet to move from the couch, but he was awake and sitting up now, and whatever she'd brewed up seemed to be doing the trick. His blisters had all but healed, the normal color returning to his face, and his eyes had regained their sharp focus.

His hands still trembled around the mug, though, and his voice was weak and watery.

"Hunters," he went on.

He told us the story of his ambush, then pointed to his inner arm. "Both had brands that matched one of the runes I'd seen on the witches' bodies in the morgue."

"What did it look like?" Emilio asked. As Darius described it, Emilio tapped out a text, presumably to Elena. She'd gone to the station to regroup with her team, and we'd promised to keep her in the loop.

"I had no choice but to kill them," Darius said.

"There is always a choice, vampire," Liam said, running his finger along one of Elena's bookshelves.

"Yes, and my choice was to not die at the hands of hunters. One I'm sure you'd make under similar circumstances."

"I wouldn't find myself in such circumstances." Liam pulled out an encyclopedia and began flipping through it, turning his back to us as if our conversation was suddenly distracting him from his studies or something.

Fucking Death.

"Everything is a bit of a blur after that," Darius continued, "but I remember feeling a terrible thirst, like nothing I'd ever felt before." A shadow darkened his eyes, and he closed them as if he didn't want Emilio or me to see it. "It just... took over. I was utterly consumed; I couldn't have stopped even if I'd wanted to."

I dropped into the chair across from him, shaking my head. "Fucking hell, Beaumont. You could've died."

"I'm quite aware of that, yes." He took another sip of Elena's brew, then set the mug on the side table, nearly dropping it in the process. "But here I am. And worry not; when I came to, I had the wherewithal to call for a clean-up."

"But not the wherewithal to stick around, where you were safely out of the sun?"

"My associates don't require supervision."

"No, but apparently you do," I said. Anger pulsed through my veins. We could have lost him. *Gray* could've lost him. "What the fuck were you thinking? Why didn't you call us?"

"I did. Many times." His voice had turned cold, but it couldn't hide the concern in his eyes. "I couldn't reach either of you."

Emilio and I checked our phones. Neither of us showed any missed calls or texts.

"We've been texting you all morning," Ronan said.

"I also left voicemails," Emilio added. "We assumed you were sleeping."

Darius pulled out his phone, staring blankly at the screen, jamming his finger into it and growing increasingly frustrated.

Taking it out of his hands, I read the notifications. "Seventeen missed texts, four missed calls. Yeah, that's us." I swiped over to his call and text log, seeing the long list of phone numbers that he'd obviously entered manually—and incorrectly. "I sure as hell hope you didn't leave anything incriminating in those messages, because you didn't leave them for us. You really need to learn how to use this thing, Beaumont."

I tossed it back to him. He caught it with one hand. At least his reflexes were improving.

"Nevertheless," he said, "the important thing is that we're together now and all accounted for, save for our missing companions. I don't suppose you have news?"

"We've... got nothing," I admitted. The words hurt on the way out. After working things out with Elena's wolf pups, we all decided it was better to wait until dark before

Emilio and I made a move. Her men were supposed to be setting up stake-outs on some of the known locations of the hunters who'd recently moved to the Cape, but I wasn't a hundred percent sure we could trust them yet.

With no sign of the victims and no solid leads, there wasn't much we could do but wait, anyway. I knew that, logically. I'd agreed to it. But I couldn't help feeling like we were failing Gray and Ash. They'd been gone nearly two days already. Who knew what kind of fucked-up torments Jonathan had subjected them to?

My only solace was that my witch and my best friend were in it together. No matter how much they pretended to hate each other, I knew there was a bond forming there. As long as it was within their power to do so, they'd do whatever they could to keep each other safe.

Darius finished the rest of his brew, then held the cup in his lap, tapping the rim with his fingers. He seemed to be considering his next words.

"I don't know how exactly to explain this," he finally said, "but I picked up on her presence today. Through our blood bond."

"*And?*" I was out of my chair, my heart pumping new blood into my veins.

"Her magic called to me, in a way. She's definitely alive, Ronan. But she's not in the Cape. She's not even *here* at all."

"What are you talking about?" I asked. "Where the fuck is she?"

"Another realm, perhaps. Maybe her own. Maybe someone else's."

I hated the question that slithered into my head next, but I let the words fall out of my mouth anyway.

"Then how do you know she's even alive?"

I looked into his eyes, everything in me silently begging him. *Please convince me. Convince me our girl is okay. That we're going to find a way to bring her back to us. That we can end her suffering, end this nightmare before it's too late...*

Darius was soundless. Not just quiet, not just silent, but utterly fucking soundless.

Until he exploded.

The mug shattered on the hardwood floor, and he had me against the wall before I could even blink.

"Bloody hell, demon. I can *feel* her. She's very much alive. But if we don't figure out how to get her out of whatever mess she's in, she won't stay that way much longer. *That* I can promise you."

"I'm afraid the vampire is right." Unperturbed by the whole scuffle, Liam slid Elena's book back into place on the shelf. Then, with a sigh so heavy I felt it land on my shoulders, he said, "You two... had better sit down."

FOURTEEN

LIAM

The demon looked more surly and terrible than usual, with bloodshot eyes and a heaviness to his gait that made his boots scuff the floor when he walked.

The vampire seemed to be recovering, albeit slowly; a slight tremor remained, and the effort of attacking his friend seemed to have taken another toll on him.

Both men sat on the couch, looking up at me almost like children awaiting news of their punishment.

To say I wasn't looking forward to this conversation was a serious understatement, but I couldn't put it off any longer. I'd already lost hours getting back to the material plane; it was becoming more difficult to transition between my forms, and the human vessel made travel much more challenging. For Gray, it'd likely been days since I'd left her. I hated the thought of her wandering the realm without me, hated knowing some of the horrors she'd likely face.

Hated knowing that the hunter was still after her, even there.

"I have connected with Gray," I finally said. "She sends a message."

"What the *fuck?*" Ronan was on his feet again. "And you're waiting until *now* to tell us?"

"It seemed wise to wait until the female shifter was gone," I said, though in truth I'd been avoiding it. Despite Gray's many assurances to the contrary, I'd failed her, utterly and completely. How could I admit to such a gross dereliction of duty? Such a breach of trust and friendship?

"What... what happened?" Ronan asked, struggling to speak. Emotion had taken hold. "Why... Is she... How is she?"

How was she? I would not use words like *well* or *alive*, for Gray was neither of those things—not by their strictest definitions. But she was present. Relatively whole, though I had no idea how long that would last.

Sidestepping the question altogether, I said, "She is trapped in the Shadowrealm."

"*What?*" he roared. I sensed he was holding back from attacking me. His arms shook with the effort, his eyes already turning black.

"How did this happen?" the vampire demanded, his tone even more accusatory than the demon's, though he hadn't risen from the couch. "What have you done, reaper?"

Fresh anger bubbled inside my vessel, filling me with hot rage. "She condemned *herself* the moment she chose to banish the hunter's soul. In fact, one might say she condemned herself the moment she refused my invitation for proper training after the first ripple of her power called across the realms to me. No Shadowborn has ever refused the call."

From the corner of my eye, I sensed movement—no more than a blur, really—and then the demon was on me, slamming me to the floor.

Even in human form, I could've destroyed him. Snuffed him out with the snap of my fingers and settled up the debt for his soul with the Prince of Hell later. Perhaps it would've been worth incurring Sebastian's notorious wrath.

But I wouldn't do it. Gray loved this demon. He was important to me by extension, whether I liked him or not. As were the vampire, the wolf, and the incubus.

"What is she to you?" the demon demanded, his hands fisting my shirt, his face so close to mine I nearly fell into the bottomless darkness of his black eyes. "What do you want with her?"

"That is neither relevant nor—"

"She's in the fucking Shadowrealm—your domain! I'd say that's *damn* relevant!"

"I was supposed to help her manifest her powers and realize her full potential through rigorous training and education—*that's* what I wanted with her. Perhaps you'll remember that the next time you try to dissuade a Shadow-born from fulfilling her—"

The force of Ronan's punch would've crushed my

vessel's skull. Fortunately for me, he'd hit the floor next to my head instead, cratering the wood.

"Shit," the wolf said, grabbing the back of Ronan's shirt and hauling him to his feet. "That's *definitely* going on our tab."

"Along with the mug I broke," Darius said.

"And the wainscoting I destroyed this morning," Emilio said, exasperated. "Guys, what are we doing? Gray's trapped in that place and we're here, breaking my sister's things, taking orders from her pack, and crawling the damn walls. We need to stop arguing and figure this out. Everyone just... just take a deep fucking breath."

Whether he'd run out of steam or realized that his violence would not bring his beloved witch back to us, I had no idea. But Ronan did as his friend asked, then offered a hand to help me from the floor.

I took it as a show of faith. Besides, his attack hadn't done any real damage.

If I'd been at my full strength, he wouldn't have been able to attack me at all, but that was a problem for another time.

"Every minute I spend here is like days to her," I said calmly, brushing the dirt from Liam's—my—clothing. "So like the wolf said, I suggest we put away this petty squabbling and focus on helping her."

"Agreed," Ronan said. "When do we leave?"

"*We* don't," I said. "*I'll* be returning to the Shadowrealm to protect her while she searches for a gateway to her own realm, and you'll be here awaiting word. I've come only to deliver her message."

We all sat down, and I told them everything she'd shared about the prison and the hunter's ultimate plans, leaving out the part about how she'd miraculously cured the incubus of his devil's trap allergy. Recalling the way her cheeks had flamed when she'd mentioned that part of the story earlier made my vessel behave in ways that I didn't care to reveal. "She wanted to be sure the others were rescued. That was her primary concern. The reason she stole the hunter's soul in the first place."

Ronan offered a brusque nod, but I didn't think he'd heard a word I'd said about the prison. He was entirely focused on Gray.

I couldn't blame him. Perhaps if I'd been more focused, she wouldn't be in her current predicament.

"You say she's fully manifested there," he said. "How long can she survive like that?"

"I don't know. To my knowledge, no one has ever physically manifested there before."

"And her idea about the connected realms and her gateway," the vampire asked. "Is that truly a possibility for escape?"

"In theory," I replied, "if Gray could find her rune gate or even another gateway to the black forest, she might be able to get back to her realm, and then back to us. It's unproven, pure speculation, but—"

"But when has Gray ever followed the rules?" the wolf

asked, affection shining in his eyes. "Even the rules of physics."

"She'll find the damn gateway," Ronan said. "Or she'll create a new one. You said it yourself, she's the most powerful Shadowborn you've ever encountered."

"She is," I said. "But you must realize that a working gateway could very well be the equivalent of three thousand miles away from her current location, and distance is the least of her challenges. She'll have no way of knowing whether the gateway will actually lead her to her intended destination, or merely to another inhospitable landscape." I stood up and began to pace, my concern for Gray manifesting in a nervous, buzzing energy that made my vessel's heart palpitate, my hands and feet tingling with pins and needles. "The realm is constantly evolving, constantly reshaping to suit the requirements for each soul passing through. Because Gray isn't there as a result of her natural death, her situation is completely unstable.

"To further complicate matters, hours passing on earth can be days or weeks in the realm. The more time she spends there, the more her mind will deteriorate. The human brain simply wasn't built to withstand the soul challenges of the realm. Her magic will become both less effective and more unpredictable. She will begin to doubt her very own eyes, her sense of smell, her intuition, her memories, and even her magic."

Emilio dropped his head into his hands, letting out a deep sigh. "And she's all alone in that Godforsaken place."

"Alone? Oh, no. Her situation is even more dire than

that." I stopped pacing and met his eyes. "The hunter has physically manifested as well."

"Wait," Ronan said. "Let me get this straight. Gray attacked Jonathan with the intention of ripping out his soul and banishing him to the Shadowrealm, but instead of their souls traveling and their bodies staying behind, they both ended up there, fully formed?"

I nodded.

"And now she's in a strange and unpredictable realm with no clear way out," he went on, "facing violent beasts and unnavigable landscapes, diminished mental capacity that may or may not include hallucinations, and unpredictable magic. On top of all that, the bastard who basically killed her mother, stalked her for a decade, murdered her best friend, and kidnapped and tortured her is now hunting her in that place, with none of us there to protect her?"

"That is an accurate summary," I said.

The three men exchanged glances I couldn't even begin to decipher.

The demon rose from his chair once again, only this time, it wasn't to attack me.

Turning to the vampire, he held out a hand and said, "Pop a vitamin and pack your bags, bloodsucker. You and I are going on a road trip."

FIFTEEN

EMILIO

"She's in the damn *Shadowrealm*," I said, because Liam had left to rejoin Gray, and it seemed I was the only one left in this house with an ounce of good sense. Ronan and Darius were so hell-bent on rescuing Gray, they hadn't stopped to consider a very obvious point: they had no way to get to her without killing themselves first.

"All the more reason for us to move on this now," Ronan said. "I don't want her stuck in that nightmare for another minute, let alone days or weeks."

"Neither do I, but that doesn't change the fact that you can't get there unless you're dead."

"Not true." Ronan's jaw was tight, his eyes flat and grim. "There's another way."

I knew immediately where his mind had traveled.

"You can't be serious," I said. Then, to Darius, "He can't be serious."

Ronan shoved a couple of bottled waters from my sister's fridge into a bag, then helped himself to an apple. Taking a big, sloppy bite, he said, "I'll give you two minutes to talk me out of it, wolf."

"I don't need two minutes to remind you that Sebastian is *not* your ally." If he thought the Prince of Hell was out to do him any favors, then he needed medical attention, because Detective Hobb's hit this morning had clearly left him with a severe concussion.

"You're not wrong," he said. "Doesn't change the fact that he's the only one who can get us there while we're still alive."

"Wait. The hell portal? You're talking about the goddamn *hell* portal?" I couldn't believe he and Darius were actually considering this. "What the fuck, Ronan? What if it spits you out in some other dimension? What if you get trapped between realms? What if something goes wrong and you end up in Oblivion?"

"Unless you know anyone else with a gateway into the Shadowrealm," he said, entirely too calm about this, "that's our route."

"Sebastian will never go for it. Not without a whole lot of fucking strings attached." I slammed my palm against the wall, rattling Elena's generic art. At this rate, I'd owe her a whole new house at the end of all this. "You should know better than anyone that making a deal with him will—"

"Making a deal with him will get us to Gray. I will make

whatever the fuck deal he wants. She's all that matters, Alvarez. Period, exclamation point, end of discussion."

"I concur," said Darius, before I could plead my case to him.

The two of them continued to pack up their supplies. It was clear I didn't stand a chance at reasoning with them.

So I'd do the next best thing.

"Where are you going?" Ronan asked as I headed into the hall closet. When I emerged with a backpack, he shook his head vehemently. "No. No fucking way, wolf."

"You're asking the Prince of Hell for express tickets to the Shadowrealm, and you think I'm just gonna stand on the pier, wave my dainty little handkerchief, and wish you bon voyage?"

"Do whatever you want with your dainty handkerchief. You're not coming with us."

I set the backpack on the kitchen counter and loaded it up with a few more things from my sister's kitchen. "You keep telling yourself that."

He grabbed the pack and shoved it under the sink, slamming the cupboard door in front of it. "I said, you're not coming with us."

"Damn it, Ronan!" I roared. "I lost her too!"

No, Gray and I hadn't known each other as long as she and Ronan had, but that didn't make it any easier to know she was in danger, trapped in a strange, otherworldly realm with no connection to any of us. I was losing my mind inside, torn between my concern for her and my desire to utterly *shred* the hunter who'd set this whole thing in motion.

From the moment she'd turned up in the Bay, the need to protect her had called to a deep, primal part of me. The feeling had only intensified after we'd started spending time together after Sophie's murder, and once Gray had been taken from us, an unquenchable fire burned inside me, ready to consume everything in its wake if I let my guard down for even a minute.

So if Ronan and Darius truly believed that Sebastian would help them get to the Shadowrealm—if they were willing to risk their lives in the hell portal for a shot at saving Gray—then I was damn well going with them.

"You can try to stop me," I warned, a growl rumbling through my chest, "but you'll definitely get hurt."

Ronan grabbed my shoulders, his brow creased with concern. "*You'll* get hurt, Alvarez. That's the whole fucking point. You may be a shifter, but you're still human on the inside. Your *soul* is still human. You can't risk going into the Shadowrealm alive—you won't make it out."

"And you and Darius will?"

"Probably not, but we don't have human souls to worry about. Sebastian already owns mine, anyway."

"Furthermore," Darius added, "we still haven't located Asher and the missing witches. If they're still being held here in Raven's Cape, we're counting on you to track them down and bring them home."

"Darius isn't fully recovered," I said, as though that would make a damn bit of difference to either of them.

"Even at my weakest, *El Lobo*," Darius said, "I'm stronger than that hunter."

"You aren't winning this argument, brother." Ronan smacked my chest, then gave my cheek a few affectionate slaps. "Stop thinking with your big dumb heart and start thinking with your head."

Sonofabitch.

Ronan and Darius were right.

Yes, my first instinct was to protect Gray. But instinct had to be tempered with logic. And right now, despite all the fire in my gut and the itch under my skin urging me to follow them, logic was telling me that my place was here in Raven's Cape, working the other side of the case. Elena and I, along with her pack, needed to focus on getting Asher and the witches out of that prison and bringing down the hunters and dark fae behind it.

Resigned, I gripped Ronan's shoulder, an apology and a blessing all in one. "Bring her back, demon."

He nodded once, the determination in his eyes telling me everything I needed to know.

Ronan *would* bring her back. Or he wouldn't be coming back at all.

They packed up the last of their supplies, and then it was time. Darkness had fallen over the Cape, and Darius had already made arrangements with his pilot for the short flight to Las Vegas. The jet would be meeting them at the airfield shortly.

In one last-ditch effort to talk some sense into them, I said, "You do realize that Sebastian's going to have a complete fucking meltdown when he finds out she's gone, right?"

Ronan clamped a hand over my shoulder and flashed me the same devilish grin that had probably made Gray fall in love with him in the first place. "Oh, I'm *counting* on it."

SIXTEEN

RONAN

"The hell portal?" Sebastian sucked bourbon through his teeth, then hissed. "I'm not Uber, son. You do not avail yourself of my portal whenever the mood strikes."

"I'm not sure you're getting the urgency here," I said, staring out the floor-to-ceiling windows that stretched across one side of his office. The strip was lit up in its usual carnival glory. "Gray was kidnapped by a hunter a few days ago. She has since sacrificed herself in order to banish his soul to the Shadowrealm."

"So you've said. And this requires the use of my portal, not to mention my valuable time and that of my staff, because...?"

I turned away from the glittering view to face him. He sat in his leather chair like a real king of the castle, a drink in one hand, his other smoothing down what remained of his limp, gray hair.

He'd replaced the desk I'd destroyed on my last visit

with a glass table—not the smartest choice, since I was already imagining the sound it would make when I threw his ass right through it.

Also, I could see everything going on below it.

Like the fact that his zipper was open, his white boxers marked with a ring of bright pink lipstick that matched that of the woman who'd shown us in. And that his rug was scorched, suggesting he'd recently banished a demon to Oblivion on that very spot where his table now hovered.

More importantly, I could see his knee bobbing.

He could play it cool all he wanted. Fact was, talk of Gray and the Shadowrealm was making the Prince of Hell very, very nervous.

I shot a quick glance at Darius, who'd been silently standing by the door the entire time. That alone was enough to make anyone nervous, but Sebastian had a particular disdain for vampires.

Probably because he couldn't control them.

"By violating the natural order of the universe," I continued, since apparently he needed someone to connect the damn dots for him, "she has condemned her own soul to the realm." I gave him a few seconds to process all that before adding, "Eternally."

Bullseye.

I'd finally hit the mark with that one. All the signs were there: the bobbing knee, the slight twitch of his mustache, the pulse of the vein in his forehead.

T-minus ten seconds to core meltdown...

"It seems she finally found the loophole in her contract," I said, giving him that last little push over the edge.

Right on cue, the man exploded.

"How could you let this happen?" he shouted, slamming his bourbon glass down on the table. The glass shattered, leaking booze and ice all over his paperwork, but he ignored it.

Folding my arms across my chest, I gave him a casual shrug. I could play cool and collected, too. Especially if it made him lose his shit. The more frantic he became, the easier he was to manipulate.

"That's a question for Gray," I said. "Not for me. But as you can see, she's not here."

He was out of his chair with rage, jabbing a finger into the air. "You were charged with guarding her, boy. Not fucking her!"

At this, Darius stepped forward, capturing Sebastian's attention without a word. Darius crossed the room to the mahogany bar and helped himself to a glass of whiskey, no ice.

Keeping his eyes locked on Sebastian's, Darius raised his glass and nodded. "Please. Continue."

"She... she is demon sworn," he said, collecting his anger and settling back into his chair. "Sworn to *me*. And has been for a very long time."

"I don't know what to tell you, Sebastian," I said. "She did what she had to do, and now she's gone, body and soul."

"*Body?*" Sebastian went damn near purple with rage

again. "You're telling me she's still *alive?* In the fucking Shadowrealm?"

"That is our understanding, yes," Darius said.

"But that's impossible. The prophecy—" He cut himself off abruptly, suddenly busying himself with the wet papers on his table. The P-word hung in the air between us.

Darius caught my eye, giving me a slight nod. He'd heard it too. Wondered.

Centuries old and mistranslated many times over, the prophecy itself had become little more than a spooky folk-tale trotted out on Halloween, complete with all the usual superstitious flair—take a third daughter of a third daughter of a third daughter, mix in a witch born under a full moon at the stroke of midnight, add in a little doom and gloom about the end of the world and a pinch of dried batwing, and stir.

But from its alleged origins in the Silversbane scrolls— some of the very first records of the craft—the core of it had remained the same. Strip away all the trappings and misin-terpretations, and here's what you got: a powerful Shadow-born witch foretold to unite the fractured covens against a devastating threat.

Sebastian had always said he didn't believe in the Silversbane prophecy, or that it had anything to do with Gray. His reasons for wanting her soul had more to do with what others believed, and the power he'd gain from owning something perceived as so highly valuable.

Or so he'd claimed.

I'd always had my suspicions. From the moment I'd first

seen her, it was clear she was born for more than a life in the shadows.

But with that one little slip-up, Sebastian had just shown us his cards.

He believed the prophecy was about Gray. And he couldn't wait to claim her soul—to put a powerful witch to work to *his* ends.

My hands clenched into fists at my sides. No matter how many times a day I thought about her damn contract, I still couldn't accept it.

When Sebastian finally looked up from his table again, his face was a mask of forced control. "In any case, I don't see why you insist on raising my blood pressure, son. So she's in the Shadowrealm. She'll finish her trials and be delivered straight to me. Nothing can break her contract."

"I used to believe that, too," I said. "But she is, after all, a Shadowborn. Quite unpredictable. Extremely powerful. If I'd known that when you'd first assigned me to her, this whole scenario might've turned out differently."

"This is not acceptable!" he bellowed, stabbing his finger into the glass table. "Demon sworn can *not* make deals with any other being. She is mine, no matter what your so-called natural order dictates."

"If you're quite finished," Darius said, taking a fresh glass from the bar and pouring Sebastian another drink, "we'd like to discuss our options for bringing her back."

"There's no *our* in this, bloodsucker. Gray is mine."

"Really? Then by all means." Darius handed him the drink and bowed over his desk. "Retrieve her."

He blustered awhile longer, but eventually, he came around and shut his mouth.

Just like I knew he would.

"We need passage through the hell portal," I said. "Once we're in the Shadowrealm, we'll track her down and help get her back to the material plane."

"I want my property returned," he said. "Or there will be hell to pay."

"Why do you care so much about one witch's soul?" Darius asked.

"*Aside* from the fact that she's my property?" Sebastian sipped his bourbon. "Let's say you rescue her from this fate, and bring her back to the world alive and unbroken. Well, you've just made her a martyr and a hero. The witch who sacrificed her eternal soul to eliminate one hunter, and then returned, resurrected. What a PR story! And what do you suppose the other witches will do when they hear of this hero? They'll..." He trailed off and shook his head. "That kind of power—real or perceived—is dangerous in the wrong hands."

"The covens have all but disbanded," Darius said. "Witches are nearly extinct. They have no real power, Sebastian, and haven't for a long time. One untrained, undisciplined witch isn't going to change that."

What a joke. Darius and I both knew that one witch could change a hell of a lot of things—Gray had already done just that. But Sebastian's mind didn't work that way. He'd slithered his way to the top of Hell's food chain, but deep down he was the same small-minded, short-sighted demon he'd always been.

"Listen, Sebastian," I said. "Frankly, we're out of options here. Either you let us pass through the portal, or you walk away from Gray's contract and move on to another witch. After all, you seem to think there are plenty left."

"Gray is the key to *everything*," he muttered, almost to himself. Then, "Tell you what, son. I believe I will allow you to pass through my portal after all. My guards will ensure you're not harmed en route."

I nodded my thanks, letting him pretend it'd been his idea all along.

I didn't give a fuck about who took the credit. I gave a fuck about saving my witch from that nightmare.

"You will retrieve the witch," he continued, "and bring her back to me, body and soul intact."

"Technically, you've only got a claim to her soul," Darius reminded him. "Upon her death, which hasn't yet come to pass. Unless I've misunderstood the terms of the contract?"

Sebastian narrowed his eyes at Darius, but then he nodded. "Very well. You shall be escorted to the portal. The guards will wait for your return to escort the three of you back to me. I'm very much looking forward to introducing myself to Gray. It's never too late to start paving the way for a good working relationship."

At that, I let out a laugh. "Yeah, I don't think so."

Sebastian knew as well as I did that bringing Gray back

through the hell portal was not an option. Darius and I could handle it, but her human soul could very easily be trapped in hell, especially since she was already sworn to him.

He was so fucking transparent.

"Darius and I will return through the portal," I said. "Gray will be exiting by a different route."

He stared at me a long time, trying on his very best poker face. He'd been trampling me most of my life, but this was one thing I wouldn't bend on, and he knew it.

He drained the last of his bourbon and sighed. "Very well, demon. I'll have my people draw up the papers for you to sign, and then you and your vampire will be on your way."

I nodded. Sebastian never made a deal without getting it in writing.

"Signatures won't be necessary," Darius said to me. "Our generous host is offering us passage through the portal as a show of good faith that we will collect Gray and return her to the material plane, so that when she ultimately passes, her soul will be his to claim, per the terms of her contract."

Sebastian laughed his oily, car-salesman laugh. "Vampire influence has no effect here, but I applaud the effort."

"That is no influence, Prince. Merely a fact." Darius offered an icy smile, then headed for the door.

"Ronan?" Sebastian asked. "A word, if you don't mind?"

I looked to Darius, then nodded.

"Don't sign anything, hellspawn," Darius warned as he

opened the office door and stepped out into the hallway. "Come find me when you're ready."

"Where you heading?"

"Poker table." Darius grinned. "Despite Sebastian's claims to the contrary, I'm betting there are still some places where vampire influence is *very* effective."

* * *

Sebastian shut his office door and turned to me, malice glinting in his eyes. "You don't even know if the witch will be able to find another exit, let alone where it will lead her."

"That's a chance we're all willing to take."

"If you fail, she'll be trapped in misery. Or worse."

"I understand the risks."

"And you speak for her, too?"

"I'm sure she'd agree with me on this."

His eyelid twitched—the only indication that this was getting under his skin. "If you change your mind, son—"

"I know how to reach you. Are we done?" I reached for the door.

"There's one more thing, demon."

"There always is, isn't there?" I blew out a tired breath, bracing myself for his usual diatribe about remembering my place.

But instead, he said, "I'm going to need something from you, too. Consider it a show of good faith."

I turned to catch his grin, shining brighter than the city lights below.

I probably should've seen it coming. Centuries doing his bidding, living under his thumb, and I still hadn't learned the most basic lesson: it didn't matter who was holding all the cards. In the end, in Vegas and in Hell, the house *always* fucking won.

* * *

I saw myself out of Sebastian's office, wishing I could shower off the greasy, unsettled feeling our conversations always left me with. But there wasn't time for that. I collected Darius from the casino, and we took a cab out past the city limits. The portal entrance was buried in the desert; we had to walk the last two miles.

Neither of us spoke. There wasn't much else to say.

The entrance was nondescript, no more than a manhole cover in the sand, hiding out in no-man's land in plain sight.

One of Sebastian's underlings was already waiting for us. He smiled the same oily smile as his boss when we arrived, gesturing for us to climb down the ladder that would lead us underground, and eventually, to the portal itself. "One at a time, gentlemen. This way, if you please."

I looked at Darius. The desert wind blew across the sand and into my face, hot and rancid even at the late hour.

It tasted like an omen.

Sebastian's words echoed.

I'm going to need something from you, too...

"Well, here we are, then." Darius grabbed me for a quick

hug, slapping me twice on the back. It was an affectionate gesture for the typically cool vampire, and I tried not to take it as a goodbye.

"See you on the other side, brother," I said.

He met my eyes once more, offering a quick nod. "Let's hope so."

SEVENTEEN

GRAY

The glass rainstorm lasted for days, leaving me trapped in the caves with nothing but my own thoughts for company. I was so desperate to feel the sun on my skin that on the first clear, silent morning, I bolted out of the cave mouth like a true bat out of hell.

But instead of hitting the boulder field Liam and I had crossed to get here, I suddenly found myself in an orchard of bright green pathways lined with perfectly manicured trees. Their flowers fluttered in the breeze like paper, each bloom buzzing with honeybees.

Passing under low-hanging branches, I realized they weren't flowers at all, but tarot cards.

One fell before me, riding a soft current down to my feet.

I picked up the card and turned it over, revealing an image of a nude couple bathing in a river beneath the romantic glow of the moon. A fairy made of pure white light hovered above them.

The man in the image reminded me of Ronan, and I smiled softly, letting the warm, loving energy of the Two of Cups wash over me. But soon the air around me chilled, and the peaceful, nurturing image on the card morphed into something else. It was still the Two of Cups, but this image was much more sinister, featuring a skeleton cornering an ebony woman in a dark, shadowy tower. Blood had been spilled on the floor between them.

They shared a toast and drank from silver goblets, but unlike the couple in the river, this couple was not in love. Fear and malice crawled over my skin like a swarm of fire ants.

Death and Midnight sitting 'neath a tree
Nothing is real but what you see
Cups over swords, blood over minds
Which will you trust — your heart or your eyes?

The words echoed in my mind as the card vanished from my hand.

On the path ahead, a man walked toward me. No more than a silhouette at first, he emerged from the center of the orchard with a determined stride.

He lifted his head and met my gaze as he approached, his smile mischievous behind a thin beard, his eyes like leaves in the autumn.

My breath caught, my feet carrying me to him of their own accord.

"*Ronan?*" I gasped, falling into his arms, but he didn't reply.

He *looked* like Ronan. Smelled like him too, filling my senses with the cloves-and-campfire scent that always reminded me of home. Of our friendship. Of everything we'd become to each other.

But when I reached up and touched his face, his smile died, and his eyes turned flat and empty in a way that sucked all the hope from my heart. I watched in mute horror as the hazel melted into solid black, then changed to a hazy gray. Slowly, wordlessly, agonizingly, the rest of his body turned to smoke in my arms and floated up into the trees.

We'd finally been reunited, and Ronan... He'd been smoked out. Obliterated.

A scream lodged itself in my throat, the pain in my chest driving me to my knees.

I hadn't even caught my breath yet when I felt the touch of another man's hand on my shoulder.

"There, there, love. No need for that."

I tilted my chin up to see my vampire, impeccably dressed in a charcoal suit, crisp white shirt, and ivory tie.

My heart was shattered. I'd just lost my best friend, the man I loved. But the sight of Darius soothed the endless ache, just long enough for me to take a breath.

"Darius," I whispered, reaching for the hand still resting on my shoulder. "He's... he's gone. Ronan is gone."

When Darius spoke again, his voice was heavy with something I didn't quite recognize. "We've been searching for you a long time, Gray. This isn't unexpected. Perhaps you shouldn't have come to this realm."

"But... this was *my* choice. My fate. I never meant for you and Ronan to follow me here."

"Intention hardly matters," he said, cool and logical as always. "We are, in fact, here."

Disappointment. That was the thing I'd heard in his voice, so unfamiliar to me.

He pulled his hand away and took a step backward. "I should probably take my leave."

"Wait!" I shot to my feet, stumbling after him. It was hard to walk; suddenly I was wearing an ivory sheath dress the same shade as his tie and a pair of nude heels. "I'm coming with you. I think... we're supposed to go somewhere?"

"I don't think so, love. We've been searching far too long, and there is still much ground to cover. I must leave."

"What are you talking about? I'm right here, Darius! You found me!" Was there something in the atmosphere affecting his perception? His mind?

He shook his head, lowering his eyes to the ground. "I'm afraid it's too late."

"It's not!"

He closed his eyes and stepped into the direct sunlight. Blackness seeped down from his head, running down his face like spilled ink.

"Darius, no!" I reached for his hands, trying to pull him into the shade beneath the tree, but he wouldn't budge.

His black skin began to smoke.

I tugged harder, yanking and jerking, begging him to move, but he was as still as a statue, rooted as a tree. I gave him one last tug, but my hands slipped, and I fell to the ground at his feet.

Blood poured from his lips, dripping onto my head, warm and sticky and terrible. Paralyzed with fear, I sat helplessly as Darius liquified before my eyes.

Dark, wet blood stained my skin. My dress. It was all that I had left of him.

Ronan and Darius were both dead.

This time I *did* scream, a primal howl that tore through my throat and out my lips, ripping me apart on the way. It was so loud, so deep, it made the trees quake, the tarot-card leaves falling all around me.

The Lovers card landed before me—another naked couple, this time on the beach, wrapped in an erotic embrace. A serpent had just sunk its fangs into the man's leg.

When I rose up from the ground and looked up the path, my gaze locked onto a pair of familiar ocean-blue eyes.

"Tears? Seriously?" Asher's cupid-bow lips stretched into a sexy grin. "I thought you'd be at least a *little* happy to see me."

"Ash!" I reached for him, but he held up a hand to stop me.

"I can't stay."

"Why?"

He shrugged. "I'm dying."

"But… how? Do you need to feed?"

"Nah. Nothing you can do about that. It's in my blood. It's killing me."

"The devil's trap? But I… I saved you. It's gone." I stretched up on my tiptoes and pressed my mouth to his, desperate to taste the cinnamon heat of his kiss. To remember what it felt like to be in his arms, falling apart at the seams in the best kind of way.

His lips were cold and unyielding.

"No, witch," he said firmly, pushing me away.

"Why are you doing this?" I whispered.

Asher shook his head, turning his back on me. "Because you're *poison*, Cupcake. And you're killing us all."

I tried to go after him, but he disappeared beneath the archway of tree branches, and another tarot card fluttered down before me. It was the High Priestess this time, dressed in her sky-blue robes and standing on a crescent moon, wielding her crystal scepter.

Remembering my mother, I reached out to touch the woman's face, but the card transformed. Unlike the dreamy, peaceful Priestess I'd just seen, the one looking up at me now was fierce and wild-looking, with two interlocking crescent moons for a face and long, skeleton-white fingers. Her dark gray wings were studded with rivets, as if they were made of metal.

The card vanished, and a woman with curly gray hair

stepped out from behind the trees. She wore an amulet—a silver crescent moon beneath an eye made of opal, topaz, and black onyx.

I'd know that amulet anywhere. She'd died wearing it. And the hunters who'd butchered her tore it from her neck.

"Calla?" I breathed. It'd been ten years since I'd seen her, but she looked just as I remembered, with sharp eyes and that wild, curly hair.

"I'm so sorry," I said. They were the first words that came to mind—ones I'd been wanting to say to her since her death.

"I know you are," Calla said with a small frown. She reached forward to fluff out my dress, which had transformed from the ivory sheath to a peach-colored sundress that just skimmed the tops of my thighs. "But sorry is just a word. It's not enough. If only you'd been stronger, Rayanne."

"I survived, though. Just like you told me to."

"Still, a capable witch would've been able to save me, too."

"But I was just a kid!"

"And yet you were already able to bring animals back from the dead." She clucked her tongue. "I never should've adopted you. You've always been broken, child. There was a reason your real mother abandoned you."

I blinked in confusion, heart hammering in my chest. "But... you told me my mother died."

"Died, abandoned you, sold you to the highest bidder... What difference does it make? You turned out terrible anyway. She should've killed you as a baby. All of us would be better for it."

"You don't mean that." I reached for her, but it was too late. Flames licked her feet, twisting their way up her legs like vines.

She glanced down, swatting absently as if shooing an annoying fly. "Now look what you've done."

I dropped to my knees and tried to tamp down the flames, but my action only seemed to aggravate them. They surged upward, brighter and stronger, crackling loudly.

My mother turned black, burning away like paper in the span of a single heartbeat. In the dusty pile of ash and bone she'd left behind, another card materialized.

Judgment.

In it, gray bodies rose from a crypt, called forth by an angel's trumpet.

Panic made my hands tremble. I knew who was coming next.

The bones of my mother reformed, the skeleton slowly filling in with flesh and hair. It wasn't like Calla's hair, though; it was dark and lanky, hanging in front of her face. She wore dirty jeans and a dark blue hoodie with a unicorn on the front.

"Bean," I gasped, the sight of her almost more than I could bear. She'd died in an alley protecting me, and I'd resurrected her by mistake, leaving her to suffer at the hands of Jonathan.

I still hadn't been able to deliver her soul to its proper resting place.

She pointed a shaking finger at me, and my peach sundress turned into a mirror image of her outfit. "You did this to me, witch."

"I know, and I'm so, so sorry. If I could take it back, I would."

"You can't, though. You can't take anything back."

"Bean, wait. Let me help you. Let me free your soul." I reached for her, but the moment my fingers brushed her sleeve, she disintegrated, blowing away on the breeze.

In the grass where she'd stood, another card bloomed like a flower.

I plucked it from its stem, looking at the beautiful ebony-skinned girl on the front, carrying a fish in a golden cup. The youthful, vibrant energy of the Page of Cups had always reminded me of Sophie, and I sighed in relief at the sight of it. Sophie would help me through this. She'd been with me always, and I needed her now, more than ever.

"Sophie?" I called out.

She materialized before me, leaning against the trunk of a tree, casually inspecting her fingernails. They'd been painted white, with tiny pink dots. Her skin was painted with blue-green swirls, just like it'd been the last time I'd seen her alive.

My jeans and hoodie transformed into a black linen dress and veil, like some kind of funeral attire.

"It should've been you, you know," she said with a shrug. "Your boyfriend killed me. You led him right to me, just like you led him to your mother."

"Sophie, no! I didn't know."

"You should have, though. That's the thing." She shrugged, and the swirls painted on her chest transformed into runes carved brutally into her skin. They ignited one at time, glowing as bright as candle flame.

"I would do anything to change it," I said. "To save you."

"That's what everyone says." She rolled her eyes, then blew on her polka-dot fingernails. "Nice seeing you again, Gray. Take care of yourself, okay?"

She turned to go, but I grabbed her from behind, tackling her down to the ground and pulling her into my lap like a baby. Everyone else got away from me, but she wouldn't. Not like this. She struggled hard, bucking and kicking, but I locked my arms around her and held on tight, pressing my lips to her ear.

"Shh. Listen to me," I pleaded. "Just listen."

Sophie finally stilled. I tore the veil from my eyes and looked down at her again, but Sophie was gone. The warm body in my lap was now a newborn fawn, shivering and bloody. An arrow pierced his neck.

"Oh no!" Gently, I reached for the arrow, trying to see if I could push it all the way through, but the poor creature howled in agony. "I'm sorry. I don't know what to do."

"You've done enough," the fawn sputtered, his blood dripping onto my bare thighs. Then he became a wolf.

My wolf.

Emilio shifted into his human form, naked and feverish, his body wracked with pain.

"Gray?" He blinked up at me, his eyes wide with shock,

the arrow lodged deep in his throat. "How could you do it?"

Tears leaked from my eyes, dripping onto his face. "I didn't know."

He stared at me for a long, agonizing moment before speaking again, his voice as thin as the breeze. "You betrayed me. You betrayed all of us."

"I didn't mean to! I'm so, so sorry. Just... just hang on. We'll get help. Liam is—"

"No." Emilio coughed, his chest heaving with the effort. "It's over, *querida*. Just... just let me go."

"It isn't. It isn't over! You have to be okay," I said, stroking his face. "You have to come back home with me and make brownies. There's so much I have to tell you. So much I want to ask you. Please!"

I leaned over and pressed my lips to his, desperately trying to breathe life back into his broken body, but he'd already gone cold.

Grief took hold of my heart, squeezing it until it cracked. I couldn't scream. Couldn't sob. I couldn't even breathe. I had nothing left inside.

We are, all of us, bound for darkness.

The words rung in the distance, a faint echo a thousand miles away and a million years in the past. At the time I'd said them to Liam, I believed their message was prophetic.

Now, I saw that message for what it was—a pathetic warning come much too late.

My broken heart slowed. I could feel the blood thickening inside me, my magic leaking out through my limbs.

There was nothing I could do to stop it. To stop any of this.

The breeze slipped through the orchard, rustling the leaves and gliding over my skin, lifting the hair off my neck. It carried with it a hundred tarot cards, each one turning into a whisper that fluttered against my ears, cruel and cold and true.

You failed him.

You failed all of them.

You are a failure, a death-bringer, a dark pit of despair from which there is no escape.

You don't deserve to live.

I fought off a shiver and closed my eyes, trying to remind myself that I was still human. That I *did* deserve to live, even though I'd made so many mistakes. So many things I couldn't repair or take back.

But truth was the sharpest weapon in any arsenal, relentless in its pursuit. It pried open my chest, sliced my heart into ribbons.

He would still be alive if not for you.

They probably wish they never met you.

Your rebels would be better off without you. The witches would be better off without you. The world would be better off.

End it.

End it, Gray Desario.

End it. End it end it end it end it end it end it end it —

"No! Leave me alone!" I curled up on the ground in agony, but no matter how bad the pain, I wouldn't do it. I wouldn't give up like that. I wouldn't let my regrets and doubts consume me.

I would live. I would walk away from this.

Even if it meant I'd spend the rest of eternity nursing this wound.

It was mine to carry. Mine to nurture. Mine to remember.

"You can't have me!" I screamed at the trees, my cries echoing across the orchard.

Everywhere my tears soaked into the earth, a pale yellow flower bloomed, then rotted, its cloying scent making the back of my throat itch.

"Fuck you!" I shouted. "Fuck everything about this place!"

The touch of a strong, broad hand on the back of my head pulled me from the desperation.

I sat up again, looking straight into Ronan's coal-black demon eyes.

Now, I was naked, and he knelt beside me, running his hand down my bare backside.

I sighed at his tender touch, wanting to lose myself in it.

"It's okay," he said, stroking my skin. "It'll all be over soon."

Ronan turned to smoke.

And the torture began anew.

Endlessly I relived each torment, each regret, each mistake. The scenarios played out differently—sometimes Darius was beheaded instead of incinerated, sometimes my tongue was carved with the devil's trap that banished

Ronan's soul. I watched Emilio shoot Bean, watched my mother skin Emilio alive, watched Sophie dance on Asher's bloody corpse—but they always ended the same way.

Everyone I'd ever cared about was dead. Because of me.

Each loss hit me all over again, as fresh and sharp as if it'd never happened before. And each time they reappeared, their presence filled my heart with hope, as if *this* time might finally be the one to end this nightmare.

As if all of the people I'd so terribly wronged might finally forgive me—might finally live.

But they never did.

I spent days in the orchard, lying naked on a blanket of rotten yellow blooms and tattered, ever-changing tarot cards.

"Let me go," I whispered, over and over, each time the loop began again.

But it never worked. No matter how much I begged, the ghosts of my past wouldn't let me go.

Eventually, the parade of death and regret blurred, and a thick, billowy fog crept across the orchard, enveloping me in a white haze, slowly dissolving my body until there was nothing left of me but a whisper on the wind.

In the end, that was silenced, too.

Breathe, Gray. Just breathe…

I was suspending in nothingness, a momentary reprieve. And there, in the spaces between, I found my way out of the orchard.

I had to let them go. It was that simple—and that difficult.

I opened my eyes and returned to my body, still lying naked in the patch of rotten flowers. The mist had retreated. The ghosts of my past had returned, all of them watching me as if waiting to see what I'd do next.

Slowly, I got to my feet and took a deep breath.

Then, without another word, I turned my back on Darius, Ronan, Asher, Sophie, Emilio, Bean, and even the mother I missed more than anything in the world, and I walked away.

The orchard vanished behind me, and I followed the pull of my magic toward the sound of the ocean, feeling lighter for the first time in a long time.

One thing had become clear. Alive or dead or somewhere in between, I didn't belong in the Shadowrealm.

I didn't care how impossible and unnatural and unheard of it was. I didn't care how far away the gateway was, or how many beasts and nightmares I might meet along the way.

All I knew in that moment was this: I was a goddamn Shadowborn witch. I was going to find some clothes. And then I was getting out of this fucking place.

EIGHTEEN

ASHER

In the weak yellow light of a single dim bulb swinging on a chain, the witches on C-block looked like ghosts in a haunted asylum.

They were all crammed into the cell together—a cold, damp chamber with no bedding or chairs. All of their heads had been shaved, the hair growing back in tufts and patches. Dressed in dirty white hospital gowns, the women were deathly pale, their bones sharp.

A few of them had bandages on their wrists and ankles. Others had... *fucking hell.*

I bit back my rage, shoving it down deep, saving it for the men who'd done this.

They were *carved*. Runes, letters, symbols, slashes—angry red lines crisscrossed arms and legs, chests, faces.

He carved their fucking faces. *Faces!*

"Asher?"

The call was soft and watery, but I recognized her voice, and my throat tightened at the sound of it.

The last time I'd seen Haley was on the back of my motorcycle in front of her house, just before we'd gotten pinched by hunters.

"Haley," I breathed, damn near gasping at the sight of the runes carved into her forehead.

I am going to kill every last hunter in this place.

"You've got some pretty sweet accommodations here," I said sarcastically, forcing a smile as she approached the bars. I didn't want her to know how truly freaked out I was by her condition—by what Jonathan had done to her. "You must know people in high places. How you holding up?"

"Fucking great, why do you ask?" She laughed, a genuine smile breaking across her gaunt face. "Shit, Ash. I've never been so happy to see a demon in all my life."

She'd lost a lot of her curves and all of her hair, but at least she still had her sense of humor.

"Don't go throwing me a parade just yet," I said. "I have no idea how I'm going to get you guys out of here."

"Just don't touch the bars," she said. "They're—"

"Fae-spelled. I got the memo." Damn things practically hummed with it. "How many of you are there?"

"Twenty-seven witches. That's all of us."

"You sure?"

"Pretty sure. Jonathan had us in separate cells at first, but he put us all together to make room for the other prisoners."

"You've seen them?"

"Reva has." Haley glanced over her shoulder at a young witch sitting against the back wall of the cell. I recognized the name—she was the teenager who'd contacted Gray through the fireplace back at the safe house.

"Reva's a shadowmancer—she can project her consciousness from one shadow to another," Haley explained. "So she can see things, spy, sometimes reach out to people if they're really receptive. The guards haven't figured it out yet. They barely notice her."

"I've only been doing it for a little while." The girl got up and walked toward the bars. Like the others, she was malnourished and pale, but she seemed steady on her feet, and her eyes were bright and alert. As far as I could tell, she'd been spared from Jonathan's carving knife. "I've been traveling all over the caves. Outside, too. I tried to talk to Gray a couple of times."

"Oh, she got your message, Reva," I said. Then, with a wink that made her smile, "Nearly burned down the house in the process."

"Sorry about that. Fire's easy because it always casts shadows."

"Don't apologize. Because of you, my friends know to look for us in Raven's Cape."

"Are the guys all okay?" Haley asked. "Where's Gray? Reva thought she was here for a little while, but she wasn't sure."

"I can't get a read on her now," Reva said.

"She was here. But she's... They're... You know what? It's a *really* long story, guys." I ran my hands along the wall surrounding the bars, looking for a keycard reader or access panel like the ones Fiona and I had found in the other chamber. "And I'll be more than happy to fill you in later. Like, over shots. In another fucking town. At some sleazy bar where we'll be singing karaoke and telling war stories about the time we iced a bunch of hunters and burned this whole place to the ground. But until then, we need to concentrate on getting the fuck out of here."

"Agreed," Haley said.

"Reva," I said, "what can you tell me about this place and the people running the show?"

"The cave system itself is massive," she said, "but the prison part is only about a mile long, and not that deep. There are a few big chambers like this, and cages, but mostly smaller cells where they keep different people and... other things."

The memories of what she'd seen haunted her eyes. Poor fucking kid.

"There's the medical lab," she went on. "That's where they do most of the experiments. A kitchen, a couple of rooms for the guards. That's about it."

"You said you'd been outside—do you know how they come in and out?"

She nodded. "There's an old pier on the beach with a fish-and-chips place that looks like it closed down a million years ago. There's no public beach access, so it's pretty isolated. The hunters come in and out through a hidden entrance underneath the pier."

"In the water?"

"Yeah, but it's not really water. It's just spelled to look that way."

"Fae magic," I said.

"Exactly."

She continued to fill me in about what she'd seen on her travels, confirming a lot of what I'd already suspected. Jonathan had a rag-tag crew of hunters and a few supers—mostly mercenaries, just like Fiona had said. They'd been nabbing witches and supers, killing some of them, bringing the others here. Jonathan was trying to create hybrids, along with various magical and biological weapons.

And now he had help from the fae.

"Do you guys know anything about a fae prick named Orendiel?" I asked.

Reva shook her head.

"Doesn't sound familiar," Haley said, "but there *have* been more fae around lately. I get the sense there's some kind of power struggle going on."

"How so?"

"At first, it was mostly just Jonathan and a few hunters. But they've been talking about someone they call 'the old man,' and I think that might be Jonathan's father. Jonathan gets real twitchy any time someone mentions him."

Snippets of the conversation I'd overheard between Shears and Smokey Joe echoed in my skull.

...the sooner the old man takes control, the better.

Kid's a fuck-up, Shears. Always has been.

Don't hold your breath waiting on the old man... He won't

make a move as long as Jonathan's alive. Can't risk the kid fucking things up with Orendiel...

This shit had coup written all over it. I didn't know jack about the old man, but if it was true what they said about apples falling from trees, he was even more dangerous than his fucked-up son.

Probably smarter than him, too, given that he'd either implanted his own people into Jon's operation, or gotten Jon's people to flip.

"Anyone got any juice left in there?" I asked the witches.

"Just Reva," Haley said. "Norah bound our active powers, and this whole place is locked tight with fae magic."

"Norah Hanson?" I asked. I'd forgotten about her. "The coven leader?"

"She's a fucking traitor," one of the other witches said, coming to stand at the bars with Haley and Reva. She was a little older—maybe mid-forties, with a husky smoker's voice and piercing yellow eyes. Her cheek was bandaged, her arms covered in bruises. "Turns out she was working with the hunters the whole time."

"Where is she now?" I asked.

The yellow-eyed woman slung a protective arm around Reva's shoulders. "We haven't seen her since she brought in Reva."

Norah was probably long gone by now.

Add that to the list of problems for another day.

"Is Gray okay, though?" Reva asked.

"She's... dealing with Jonathan."

"That fucker?" Yellow Eyes said. "Did she kill him? Tell me she killed him."

"She's... working on it," I said. In truth, I had no idea whether she'd killed him or yanked his soul into another dimension or some other crazy magical possibility I hadn't even considered. With Gray, you just never fucking knew.

Haley blew out a breath, pacing the cell. The others sat quietly along the wall or curled up on the floor, some of them comforting each other, others still in shock. Reva went back to her wall in the back and closed her eyes.

Looking to Yellow Eyes, I lowered my voice and said, "The hunters. Did any of them... Are you guys... Did they..." I shoved a hand through my hair, not sure how to say it—only knowing I was going to cut off every hunter's dick if I didn't like the answer to her question.

"No, they didn't touch us. Not like that," the woman said, and I breathed a sigh of relief. "Jonathan actually forbid it. Said some bullshit about how witches are natu-rally wonton and indecent, and if he allowed us to give in to our carnal desires, our blood would become tainted and ruin his experiments."

"That," Haley added with a snort, "and McKenna let loose an old wives' tale about turning certain body parts into certain amphibious creatures."

"Ribbit," someone replied from the shadows. McKenna, I was guessing. Several of the witches giggled. A few of them coughed.

I finally found the hidden access panel on a wall around

the corner from the cell, but it wasn't a keycard reader. It was a damn retina scanner.

"How often do the guards come down here?" I asked Haley.

"When Jonathan doesn't need us as lab rats, they only come by once a day. If that." She kicked at a moldy heel of bread on the ground. "I haven't seen anyone yet today."

Alright. We needed an eyeball, and we needed it now.

"Don't take this the wrong way, ladies, but... Which one of you do the guards hate the most?"

Haley looked over her shoulder, grinning at the witch who'd made the frog sound. "That would be McKenna. Definitely."

"McKenna?" I asked. "Think you might be up for a little shit-starting, sweetheart?"

A smile lit up her face, and she got right to her feet. "I'm your girl."

NINETEEN

GRAY

I emerged from the orchard into another world, stepping barefoot onto a sandy shore. No longer nude, I was suddenly dressed in loose cargo shorts and a purple tank top, my hair wrapped in a bandeau. Sunglasses hung from my shirt collar, and a pair of pineapple flip-flops dangled from my fingers.

This fucking place.

Still. After everything I'd just seen in the orchard, I wasn't about to complain about a walk on the beach.

A blissful turquoise sea lapped gently at my toes. They'd been painted white with pink polka-dots, reminding me of Sophie. Thankfully, the memory made me smile instead of ache.

It was a postcard-worthy moment, the bright sunshine warm and delicious on my skin, the salty air a perfect balm for my soul.

When I saw the man jogging along the shore toward me, a smile broke across my face.

"It's beautiful, isn't it?" Liam said when we met. He looked happy and relaxed, his skin tan, his hair streaked with summer highlights. Dressed in red board shorts and a faded gray T-shirt that hugged his frame, he was truly in his element.

Swimmer's build, I thought, admiring the broad shoulders and narrow waist, his muscles much more defined in the tight shirt.

"Something tells me you've spent a lot of time here," I said, pushing the blond swoop of hair out of his eyes. It was silky and warm, and I wanted to run both hands through it, but restrained myself. "It suits you."

"It suits Liam Colebrook, maybe," he said, offering a sad smile. "He loved the beach. Loved being in the water, surfing, swimming, diving, tasting the salt on his lips. All of it."

I nodded, not sure what to say to that. The more time I spent with him, the harder it was to remember that he wasn't human, wasn't just a really sweet guy I'd met on a quick getaway to California or Hawaii or some other beautiful, oceanfront paradise.

He was Death.

Again, I wondered how he did it. How he transitioned back and forth so often. How he'd existed for an eternity without any loved ones or memories or touchstones to anchor him to a specific time and place. To people.

I wanted to ask him if it was freeing, not being burdened by the pain of loss, not being caught up in the cycle of human emotion. But when I looked into his eyes now, a very human sadness peeked out from behind his usual otherworldly expression.

"This place... It's beautiful, yes. But it isn't real," he said, turning his face toward the sea. "No more than any place in the realm. It exists inside of us. Outside of us. Alongside us. Because of us. Everywhere and nowhere, all at once and not at all."

"Now *there's* the Liam we all know and love." I smiled to lighten the mood and sat down on the beach, pushing my feet into the sparkling sand. The few beaches I'd visited in Oregon and Washington had been rocky and cool, but this beach felt like spun sugar set out in the sun. "You know, I think I kind of missed you."

This got a smile, and he sat down next to me, close enough that our bare arms brushed. "And I you."

A seagull cried overhead, and I closed my eyes, losing myself in the moment. For one brief, glorious second, I could almost believe that I *had* just met Liam on the beach. That we'd come here to hang out, to talk about life, to make each other laugh as the waves rushed toward us, then away.

I nudged a little closer to him, my skin warm where our arms touched. I heard his sharp intake of breath as my knee brushed along his leg, but he didn't move away.

"I didn't mean to venture so far from the cave," I said, wondering if he'd been searching for me long. "I stepped out for some air, and I ended up... somewhere else."

"You passed through the Orchard of Echoes," he said.

"Orchard of Echoes, huh? Do they have a Yelp listing? Because that place sucked. They get *no* stars."

"No, I would think not. It preys on your fears and regrets," he continued, "slowly driving you mad with guilt. For all those who enter its paths, there are only two possible outcomes: escape, or insanity. You escaped."

"All I did was walk away."

"Indeed, that is all one *can* do. Holding on to regrets, letting our fears consume us, allowing our minds to twist them into hundreds of painful scenarios and imagined punishments—that is the path to insanity. Most who enter the orchard never realize they already know the way out, and it isn't magic or a hidden door or riddle to solve. It's simply letting go."

A chill raced across my skin, and I leaned forward, hugging my knees to my chest. I didn't want to think about the Orchard anymore.

Liam reached over and squeezed my arm. "I'm proud of you, Gray."

His touch was warm and solid, an anchor on the shore. Shielding my eyes from the sun, I turned and looked into the ancient gaze of the only friend I had in the realm.

My heart stuttered, then expanded, almost as if it was making room for something more.

"You were gone a long time," I said. "I was worried about you."

"Less than half a day on the material plane," he said. "But I know it was long for you. I hated leaving you. But I did manage to locate your—"

"The guys?" I sat up with a start. "Is everyone okay?"

"You'll be pleased to know that your vampire, your demon guardian, and your wolf have been accounted for."

"Define 'accounted for'. Be specific." I needed to know where they were. That they really were okay.

"I found them together in Raven's Cape," he said, and my heart practically sighed with relief. "Sheltering with a female wolf and her pack."

A hot, unexpected flare of jealousy cut through the relief, but I swallowed it back. It didn't matter who they were with. As long as she was on our side, the only thing I could feel for her was gratitude.

"She's Detective Alvarez's sister, if I'm not mistaken," he added, mischief glinting in his eyes. His serious expression turned into a smile, then all-out laughter, the skin around his eyes crinkling in the sun. "I see that last bit of knowledge brings you some comfort."

"Are you *messing* with me?" I returned the smile, narrowing my eyes at him. "You're messing with me. I didn't know you had it in you, Liam."

"Excuse me, but for your information, I was quite the comedian in my day."

"In your *day*?" I laughed, nudging his shoulder with mine. "Let me guess: you were the class clown of the primordial mound? Entertaining all the gods and goddesses of creation with your sparkling wit and boundless charm?"

Liam blushed, suddenly very interested in the sand in front of him.

Absently tracing a series of vertical infinity signs with his finger, he said, "They did not take the news of your banishment lightly. It seems they've made a deal with the Prince of Hell for passage through the hell portal."

"They're coming *here*?" Flashes of Darius and Ronan dying in the orchard shot through my memory, but I refused to let them take hold. None of that had been real, and I wasn't about to let those old fears consume me. Still, the idea of them following me here did not sit well. "Why didn't you stop them?"

"I would have, if they'd let me know about their plans in advance. But your vigilantes like doing things their own way, natural order be damned." He shook his head, but when he met my gaze again, he couldn't hide the spark of admiration in his eyes. "In any case, word travels quickly among hell's servants. I'm told they have already passed through the portal, but with the time fluctuations here, it will be some time before they arrive."

"How will they find us?"

"When I receive confirmation of their arrival from my sources, I will retrieve them."

"What about Emilio?"

"It isn't safe for him here. His soul his human. Demons and vampires don't have the same risks."

"I guess that's something, then." As much as I hated the idea of Ronan and Darius in the Shadowrealm, I couldn't deny the spark of warmth I felt at knowing I'd see them again. When I'd taken Jonathan's soul in the prison, I'd truly thought that was the end. That I'd never get to say goodbye. Never get to look into their eyes or press another kiss to their lips.

But now, it seemed we were all finding ways to bend the rules, creating a new reality, with or without magic.

I blew out a breath. There was still so much I didn't understand. So much left to learn about this place, about my powers, about their true limitations and consequences.

All of that would come with time—time that I was starting to believe I might just get back.

"I don't suppose there's an end game here," I said. "Or anything even *remotely* resembling a plan."

"We all want to see you returned home, Gray. That's the *only* end game."

"I thought you didn't believe it was possible."

With the palm of his hand, Liam wiped away the infinite creations he'd drawn in the sand. "You make me believe *anything* is possible."

My cheeks warmed, and that expansive feeling in my heart intensified.

"Will the hell portal stay open long enough for us to get back to it?" I asked.

"With demon's blood and the right incantation, both of which Ronan possesses, the hell portal can be opened anywhere in the Shadowrealm. When the time comes, Ronan and Darius will need to return back through it, but you must find another path." His eyes filled with something that looked a lot like sympathy. "You're demon sworn, Gray. You can't risk it."

Demon sworn. The words felt like a brand at the base of

my skull, and I wrapped my hand around my neck, trying to rub the burn out of my skin.

"Sebastian can't touch me until I'm dead. If that portal can get me back home alive, what's the issue?"

"Portal travel is highly unstable for physical beings," Liam said. "It's not unusual for a soul to separate from its vessel during the journey. It's almost always reunited upon arrival, but sometimes there's a delay. If for any reason your soul was separated from your body in the portal—for any length of time—Sebastian could trap you there, refusing to release your soul from his domain, and no one would be able to challenge him. If that were to happen, you'd be beholden to him whether you'd died or not."

"Like Ronan," I whispered, shuddering as I remembered the horrible story of Ronan's demonic enslavement. His own parents sold him out. He hadn't even been given a choice.

"We *will* find you another way home, Gray. Demon sworn or not."

"Demon sworn," I sighed. "Shadowborn. Necromancer. Violator of the Natural Order. Anything else I'm missing?"

I'd picked up so many labels on this journey, yet none of them said a thing about who I really was. I was still trying to figure that out for myself, but I was pretty sure the answer wouldn't fall under a neat little tag, like some kind of exhibit in a museum. *And over here, we have the elusive demon sworn, a rare breed of human who lost her soul to a devil's bargain made before she was even born. Now class, if you'll follow me this way...*

"Consider yourself lucky, Liam," I said. "You might try on different vessels from time to time, but at least you know who you are. Who you've *always* been."

Out on the horizon, the sun had just slipped into the sea, turning the sky the color of fire.

When the last rays had finally faded, Liam turned to me and said, "I wasn't always who I am now, Gray. I wasn't always in this form."

His hushed tone was colored with shame, as if he were sharing some deeply-guarded secret.

In that moment, I was willing to do anything to erase the haunted look from his eyes.

"Oh, I know," I teased, elbowing him gently in the ribs. "Seems like only yesterday you were terrorizing the neighborhood with your black-on-black grim creeper aesthetic."

"Gray, that's not..." He shook his head and broke our gaze, staring back out across the sea. Clearly, I'd said something wrong. The waves hushed against the shore, the silence between us stretching on for so long, my legs fell asleep.

When Liam finally spoke again, the words fell heavily— grudgingly—from his mouth. "I'm not what you think I am. Far from it."

"I'm sorry," I said. "I just meant... I don't know what I meant."

I sighed and leaned my head on his shoulder, and he scooched closer to me, wrapping an arm around my back.

It felt like forgiveness. I tried not to show how relieved I was.

"I know we've talked a lot about choice," he said, his breath stirring the top of my hair. "But the truth is, we don't always get to choose. Even when we think we have all the answers to make an informed decision."

"You're right," I said. "And you're wrong."

He laughed. "Explain. Expand. Explore."

"We don't always get to choose the things that happen to us—things other people do, or events outside of our influence, or the fact that everyone dies, or even who we love."

Liam pulled back to look at me. "You believe love is outside your influence?"

"Oh, absolutely. The heart wants what it wants, no matter how crazy or impractical or..." I thought of the men in my life right now, friends and lovers alike. "Or against the natural order it might be."

Liam blushed at that, and I took a second to gather my thoughts.

"So you're right," I said, "about things we can't choose. But we *can* choose how we deal with those unexpected things." I shrugged—that was really all I needed to say on the matter. "I chose to get out of that orchard. And I'm choosing to find a way out of this realm, no matter what the universe or anyone else has to say about it."

"And you will. I've never met anyone with as much stubborn determination and blatant disregard for the rules as you, little witch."

I leaned back on his shoulder, and Liam pressed a kiss to the top of my head, making my scalp tingle.

"This might sound completely fucked up, because... well, hello. Shadowrealm." I laughed, brushing away a tear that had slipped out. "But I'm really glad you're here with me, Liam."

"I'm glad, too, little witch." He turned and slipped his fingers beneath my chin, tilting my face up toward his and trapping me in his electric blue gaze. He watched me in silence for so long I almost didn't realize how close his lips had gotten to mine.

Almost.

He seemed to be asking a question, and I nodded in response as if he'd said it out loud.

Yes. I want this.

Liam smiled, a little bit shy and a whole lot sweet, and closed the last of the distance between us. His lips brushed mine, and we sparked.

Literally.

Both of us laughed, but neither broke away. I shifted to get closer to him, and he guided me back onto the sand, deepening our kiss.

The sparks turned into an electric current that raced down my spine and made every hair on my arms stand on end. Tiny white lights flashed on my skin wherever we touched, and overhead, streaks of lightning arced silently across the sky.

I pulled back just for a moment, looking at Liam with awe. He'd been surprising me from the moment he'd first come into my life, but never more than *this* moment, right here, right now.

Death was bursting with life.

He lowered his mouth to mine once again, and I pulled him all the way on top of me. A single touch was no longer enough to anchor me here. I needed the weight of his body against mine, the solidity, the realness. The heat.

Liam had no more words of wisdom for me, only kisses, deep and passionate and sensual, as if he were tasting chocolate and wine and all of life's most delicious flavors for the very first time. I felt him growing hard against my thigh, and I shifted and arched my hips, gasping as the firm ridge of his cock pressed against my aching clit.

He let out a soft moan, the sound of it vibrating across my lips.

"You're beautiful, Gray," he breathed, and nothing else mattered. Not the realm, not the gateway, not my eternal soul.

Only this.

When the sky turned dark, we finally came up for air. As we broke apart, a tiny spark danced across my lips, and a dozen bolts of silent lightning raced across the sky.

"Does it always do that?" I laughed, pressing my fingers to my mouth. Everything inside me was buzzing and alive.

"I was about to ask you the very same question," he said, then lowered his eyes. "I don't... I'm not... I've never done this before, Gray."

"Never?" I bit back a smile. "Not even once, borrowing a human vessel?"

Liam—older than time, vaster than the skies, etcetera, etcetera—blushed as he shook his head.

"Well, you should *definitely* get more practice, then."

"Why?" He sounded alarmed. "Was that not... satis-factory?"

"Oh, it was quite satisfactory. But you don't want to get rusty. Use it or lose it, right?"

"I'm not sure I understand what—"

"Liam?"

"Yes?"

"Can we go back to the kissing part?"

"Oh, right. Of course." He smiled, then took my face into his hands, another spark tickling my lips as we leaned back onto the sand. He'd just lowered his mouth to mine when the tide surged, dousing us both.

We sat up with a jolt, both of us laughing, our clothes clinging to our bodies, hair dripping into our eyes.

"Well," Liam said, rubbing the water from his hair. "That felt rather ominous."

The tide had returned to normal, shushing softly against the sand several feet in front of us as if it hadn't just reached up and slapped us. But the sky overhead was nearly black, flashing with lightning even though Liam and I had stopped kissing.

"I don't like the looks of that," he said now.

"Yeah, I guess it's time to go," I said, but I felt optimistic. The wave may have cooled things off between us, but it didn't feel like an ending.

Just the opposite.

There was so much more to Liam than I could've imag-ined. So much more I wanted to know. To share with him.

I was his first kiss. What other simple human pleasures had he missed out on? Had he *even* tasted chocolate and wine? Had he ever put a bathrobe on fresh out of the dryer, all warm and snuggly? Had he ever fallen asleep on the couch, only to wake up covered with a blanket that someone tucked around his shoulders? Had he ever heard blues music or run around the grass in his bare feet or gotten a back rub? Had he ever blown bubbles?

I looked at him now through new eyes, my heart beating strong and solid, a smile stretching across my lips.

I felt light. Airy. Almost... happy.

Liam stood up from the sand and held out a hand to pull me up. Despite our soaked clothes and the dark sky, the air still felt warm, carrying with it the clean, salty scent of the sea.

"I was just thinking," I said, lacing our wet fingers together. "This was actually a first for me, too."

"Bringing your emotional desires into physical manifestation with an undefinable otherworldly entity alongside an interdimensional yet largely symbolic ocean in a minuscule subdimension of a vast, unknowable realm through which all souls must pass upon the expiration of their earthly vessels in order to free themselves from the limiting psycho-spiritual binds that prevent them from reaching their eternal resting place?"

I opened my mouth. Closed it. Opened it again. "Actually, I was just gonna say 'spending the day at the beach with a hot guy.'"

"Well, I suppose that works too." Liam laughed,

pressing another electrifying kiss to my palm. "Come on, Breaker of Rules, Violator of the Natural Order, and all-around Maker of Trouble. You and I have a gateway to find."

"Okay, fine," I said, letting him lead me along the shore toward whatever the realm had in store for me next. "But as soon as we get back home, we're getting bubbles."

"What are these 'bubbles' you speak of?" he teased, but before I could answer, I watched the smile fall from his face, replaced instead with a look of sheer horror.

"Look out!" He shoved me backward so hard I fell back on the sand. Half a heartbeat later, a bolt of lightning shot from the sky and slammed into the earth where I'd just been standing, lighting up the beach like a nuclear bomb.

"Liam!" I shouted, reaching for him. But by the time I got to my feet, Liam was gone.

And I was standing at the base of a mountain in wet clothes and flip-flops in the middle of a blizzard.

TWENTY

ASHER

"If you bitches don't shut the fuck up right now," a voice boomed from down the hall, barely audible over the sound of McKenna's wailing, "I swear to God Almighty, I'll—"

Sadly, God Almighty would never know what he'd do, because as soon as Reverend Dickface rounded the corner, I bashed his pious head into the wall.

Dragging his body over to the box, I pried open his eyelid and shoved his face in front of the scanner. The reader beeped green, then displayed his name: Derrick Benson. The electronic lock on the bars snicked, the hum of fae magic dissipating immediately.

"Good eye, Benson. Thanks for looking out." Dropping the dead weight, I grabbed the bars and tugged. They slid open easily. "Haley, McKenna, help me figure out who can walk and who needs help. We need to get back to—"

Bensons' comm device beeped. I fished it out of his pants pocket and hit the answer button.

"Benson," I grunted.

"Look alive, Benson," the guy on the other end said.

Yeah, hate to disappoint you, but...

"We've got a situation on A-block," he continued. "Apparently Jon's vampire bitch set a bunch of these fuckers free. We caught her, but we've gotta lock it down up here while we round up the rest of 'em."

Damn it, Fiona.

"That all?" I barked. I needed to know whether they'd found the burnt corpses of Shears and Smokey Joe. Whether anyone had heard about my escape.

"Pretty much. Still no sign of Jon, but you know that motherfucker. Probably in a dark alley shooting himself up with shifter blood. Anyway, just sit tight down there till you hear back. Keep those bitches quiet."

"Will do," I said.

I clicked off the call, wondering how much time we had before—

The unmistakable sound of half-a-dozen pairs of boots tromping down the corridor answered that question.

Six guards, rapidly picking up the pace, all of them yammering into their comms. I caught a mention of Shears, then something about the demon getting out of his playpen.

Guess that would be me.

Quickly, I checked the stash I'd taken from Shears and Smokey Joy—the keycards, baton, lighter, stun guns, knives, flashlight, and a comm device—trying to calculate my odds. I could probably take all six of the guards, but definitely not all at once, and not fast enough to prevent them calling for backup. They had weapons, too, and who knew what else.

I couldn't risk the witches getting fucked up in the chaos.

"Everyone get back," I whispered, slipping into the cell with them and sliding the bars shut. The sound of the electronic lock snicking back into place pissed me off, but we didn't have a lot of options.

I'd be able to get the lock open again. Dead guards and eyeballs were a dime a dozen in this place. I just had to focus on the immediate crisis first—six angry, 'roided up hunters barreling down the corridor.

I ducked into the darkest part of the cell, crouching in the shadows, hoping they wouldn't spot me. The witches sat in front of me, blocking me from view just as the guards filed in.

"What the fuck happened down here?" one of them demanded. He crouched down in front of the body I'd left. "Benson? Jesus Christ."

"Who did this?" another guard bellowed.

The witches pretended to cower. "It... it was the demon," one of them said. "He was terrifying. He came down here to attack us. We called for help, and Benson came, but then the demon attacked him."

I couldn't believe the guards were buying this shit, but the lead guy turned to the others and said, "Split up. Find that incubus, or we're going to have a hell of a lot more than three dead guards on our hands." Then, to the witches, "You little cunts shut your whore mouths."

"Wait!" McKenna cried. "You can't leave us in here with that... that monster on the loose. Unlock the bars at least!"

He stepped up close, snarling. It was all I could do not to bolt for the bars and claw out his fucking eyes.

"Be grateful you're in there," he said. "If that incubus catches you outside the bars, you're gonna die with his dick up your ass, wishing Jon had let *me* fuck you instead."

Ooh, I'm gonna like killing you, fuckhole.

With those parting words and a final sneer, he left, presumably to go find the big scary incubus.

The instant he was gone, I was back on my feet.

"On a scale of one to ten," Yellow Eyes asked me, "how fucked are we?"

I considered the question. "Is ten the good end or the bad?"

"Ten is the most fucked."

"In that case, we're about a three. Maybe four," I said. "But hey, an hour ago you were an eight at least. Now you've got your very own demon—who, for the record, is actually a pretty decent guy, despite the smear campaign— a few weapons, a comm device, whatever else we can get off Benson's dead ass, and—"

"*And* a shadowmancer." Reva stepped out of the darkness at the back of the cave, grinning up at me like she was the only one in on a big, juicy secret. "I've got an idea."

TWENTY-ONE

EMILIO

Someone was watching me.

It didn't feel sinister, exactly, but even as I jogged through the desolate woods behind Elena's house, I couldn't shake the feeling that I wasn't alone.

I tried to tell myself it wasn't an omen.

It'd been days since Ronan and Darius had left for Vegas and the hell portal, and I was doing everything I could to stay focused on the case instead of worrying about them. Despite the cooperation from my sister's team, none of our leads had panned out. The hunters in town were lying low, and there hadn't been any dark fae sightings in days. We were no closer to finding Asher and the witches than we were to finding a cure for death.

I wouldn't hear news from the Shadowrealm until my brothers returned. And if they didn't return, well... I supposed I'd get a message from Liam one way or the other eventually.

But eventually was always a long damn time away when you were waiting for news about someone you cared about.

As far as we knew, no other witches had been reported missing or dead anywhere in the Pacific Northwest. But according to my guys back home, the situation in Blackmoon Bay was rapidly deteriorating, with vampire turf wars and shifter skirmishes breaking out all over the city. Illuminae, the fae club where Gray's friend Sophie had worked, decided to shut its doors for the foreseeable future after a massive brawl broke out inside the other night, destroying the bar and half the club.

We'd had our problems in the Bay over the years, but we'd kept our supernatural community under the radar. Safe, for the most part. Hidden. Now, it seemed like it was only a matter of time before some human got caught up in the mix. When that day came, all hell would break loose.

I dragged a hand across my forehead, wiping the sweat from my brow. My guys at BBPD were holding down the fort as well as they could, but there was no way I'd be able to stay out here in Raven's Cape long-term.

I hated the thought of leaving Elena, though. Something big was happening here—I could feel it in the air, like the whole place had been soaked in gasoline, and we were all just holding our breath, waiting for someone to drop the match.

The wind picked up, rustling through the pines, and I pushed myself harder, my feet thudding against the ground, sweat running down my bare back. If I could run hard enough, fast enough, maybe I could leave all those fears and doubts behind.

I ran at a punishing pace, the trees no more than a blur as I raced past them, my chest heaving with the effort, heart pounding, blood pumping, air whistling through my hair, across my skin…

I leaped over a fallen tree limb, shifting in mid-air. My wolf form came easily, effortlessly. My limbs elongated, bones popping and snapping, muscles bunching, cells rear-ranging, fur covering my skin.

By the time I hit the ground on the other side, I was on four legs instead of two and running wild, welcoming the night as it slipped over the pines like smoke.

When I'd finally outrun a few of my ghosts, I paused at a narrow stream, lapping up the cool, crisp water. I was just about to lope away when movement in the shadowy under-brush across the stream caught my eye, a gentle force pulling me toward it.

I stilled, waiting.

There it was again—a shape in the shadows, followed by a pull, like a magnet in my chest.

It looked like a girl.

It looked like Reva, the young witch from Norah Hanson's coven who'd gone missing. The one who'd reached out to Gray through the flames at the safe house.

I bounded across the stream to get a closer look, nosing around the underbrush, hoping I wasn't imagining things.

And then she appeared again, fully formed.

"Detective Alvarez," she said, flickering in and out. Then, slightly less clear, "Message… Asher."

She had a message from Asher.

I nodded, hoping she'd wait while I shifted back. I needed to be able to speak to her, to ask questions. But the moment I took my human form, she vanished.

I waited a few minutes, poking around the shadows, but she didn't reappear.

Something had caused us to lose the connection. On a hunch, I shifted back, and a minute later, I felt the magnetic pull of her again.

There she was.

As a wolf, I had access to intuition and other senses that made me much more open and receptive. But as a wolf, I couldn't talk.

Damn it. I couldn't shift back without breaking the connection. I could only hope she'd tell me what I needed to know without prompting.

I nosed the ground where I'd last seen her, where I felt the strongest pull, and she flickered back into existence, immediately launching into her message.

It was broken and garbled, fading in and out, but I caught words like Raven's Cape, Jonathan, twenty-seven witches, cave, fae magic, Asher, dozens of shifters, poisoned, dead, fae coup, guards, hunters, fish, abandoned pier.

And then the last, just before she flickered out for good —the word that made my blood run cold.

Orendiel.

Darkwinter. Sonofabitch.

Orendiel hadn't been on my radar in years, but from what I remembered, he'd been banished from the courts after killing one of the Darkwinter heirs he was supposed to be serving.

Elena had said Darkwinter were showing up in Raven's Cape. And now Reva was mentioning Orendiel. Banished or not, there was still a connection there, I was certain of it.

And, as the universe so kindly liked to remind us, there were no fucking coincidences.

* * *

"I'm telling you, Elena. She spoke to me. It's the same witch who contacted Gray through fire. It seems she's got some kind of projection magic."

Down at the Raven's Cape precinct, Elena glared at me across her desk. "Even if that were true, you said it yourself —you could barely understand her."

"Orendiel is connected to Darkwinter. That alone is worth investigating."

"Agreed, but where do we even start with that? It's just a name."

"Can you spare a couple of men to check out the piers within, say, twenty miles of the Cape?"

"Emilio. You're talking a forty- or fifty-mile stretch of beach, much of which is inaccessible during high tide, based on a garbled message from a teenager that you may or may not have even heard correctly."

"It's more than we've gotten from any other source or stakeout. It's worth checking out. If you can't spare anyone, I'll go myself."

She held my gaze another beat, then finally nodded, reaching for her phone. "Lansky. Yeah, see if you can round up Marshall and Graham. I need the three of you to follow up on a possible lead. I'll text you the details. Thanks."

She disconnected the call, sending the text then setting her phone back on the desk.

"Thank you," I said.

She nodded, not saying anything else. And I nodded, not saying anything else either.

Still, it was the longest we'd spent alone in a room together in twenty years, and I was counting that as progress.

I thanked her once more, then headed back to her place. I had my own phone call to make.

* * *

"Our source confirms that at least two dozen witches are being held, along with countless other supernaturals, all of them in poor condition. They've been beaten and tortured, starved, poisoned, and experimented on." I paced Elena's living room, the phone hot against my ear as I awaited Talia's reply to the full download I'd just given her.

My contact on the Fae Council was cold and unpleasant on the best of days, but now, even the soft sound of her breath through the phone made me shiver.

"This is all very riveting, Detective," she said, her voice toneless. "But unless I'm misunderstanding your job description, surely this falls within your purview and not the Council's?"

Her response got my hackles up, but it wasn't unexpected. The Council had been backing away from supernatural crimes for months now. Usually, that worked in our favor. I didn't need their kind of bureaucracy mucking up my cases and preventing me from doing my job.

But even with help from Elena's department, the situation here was quickly growing beyond our capabilities.

"Initially, we'd thought hunters were behind this," I said, "but it turns out they've got help." I rubbed my forehead, dreading what was coming next, still unsure whether it was the right call. Once the words were out, there'd be no taking them back.

But after what Reva had told me, I couldn't sit on this.

"It's fae, Talia," I said. "And all evidence points to Darkwinter."

She was silent so long, I thought the connection went dead. When she finally spoke, her voice was like a razor blade.

"Listen to me very carefully, Detective," she said. "Do not speak another word of this to anyone, especially on an unsecured line. To do so could be very dangerous."

"I understand that, but—"

"These are not fae to be trifled with."

"I can't sit on this, Talia. Council blessing or not. Too many people have died or gone missing. And whatever's going on in that prison? It's about to blow up in a big way. You know this."

Another icy pause. And then, "Are you still in Raven's Cape?"

"Yes."

"We will meet at nine p.m. tomorrow at the Hannaford Distillery and discuss this in person. Until then, you will not utter a word about it to anyone."

"And in the mean time?" I asked. "What about the prisoners? You're asking me to sit on my hands for twenty-four hours while—"

I was met with dead air. Talia had already disconnected the call, knowing damn well I wouldn't refuse her order.

Knowing damn well I'd take it for what it was—a threat.

TWENTY-TWO

GRAY

"Wish."

The word arrived with a gust of winter wind, buffeting my face.

"Wish. Wish. Wish."

I didn't know who'd spoken it; only that it was meant for me. I could feel it in my bones, just like the strange compulsion that pushed me onward through the snow, despite the ache in my limbs. The mountain was imposing, the summit still hidden in the clouds, but I couldn't stop—not until I reached the top.

There was something I needed up there—I was certain of it. Something that would help me find the gateway. Help me get back home.

I had to trust it.

Protective gear now covered my body, but the bite of the wind still stung, and my face was bare. Where I'd once felt the heat of Liam's kiss, now there was only frostbite. My

203

hair, which had been wet from the beach when I'd arrived, was frozen into icy dreadlocks that clicked as I walked.

High on a pass blanketed with snow and ice, I took another step forward, my boots crunching on the surface. I'd already been climbing for hours, battling the frigid temperatures and thin air that hurt to breathe, but I was so, so close.

"Wish. Wish. Die, wish."

The words were clearer now. Sharper. But I still couldn't decipher their message.

I scanned the skies for signs of more demons, but saw only the falling snow, swirling and gusting, settling on the mountaintops around me like frosting on a cake.

"Wish."

I had to keep walking. The summit loomed above. Snow and ice stung my face, but I pushed on, one foot in front of the other. Breathing was nearly impossible at this altitude; it felt like trying to suck air through a cocktail straw. For every step I took, I had to stop a moment to catch my breath.

Just one more step, I told myself. *One more.*

A wave of dizziness washed over me, but I couldn't stop. I was so, so close.

One more.

I don't know how many times I said it before it was actually true. On a steep, rocky slope slick with ice and snow, I scrambled up the last hundred feet on all fours, finally punching through the cloud cover and hauling myself up onto the very top.

The summit itself was flat and open, and much larger than I expected—about the size of a basketball court. In every direction, a thick blanket of clouds stretched as far as the eye could see, broken only by the jagged peaks of other mountains. I wondered if there were other climbers reaching their own summits. I wondered what they'd find.

"Wish."

A flash of silver in the snow caught my eye, and I crouched down to investigate. Sweeping away the snow at my feet, I revealed a slim silver dagger, it's sheath decorated with jewels.

I picked it up for a closer look, but I already knew what I'd find. It was Sophie's dagger—the one she'd left me to activate the blood spell protecting her book of shadows.

It warmed in my hand, beautiful and elegant. I was sure this was the object I'd been sent to retrieve—it felt right, and a sense of completion washed over me.

But why? Why did I need her dagger?

The wind stopped, everything around me going absolutely still and silent.

I felt like the very last person alive.

In the absence of all other sounds, the voice that came again was loud and clear.

"You die, wish."

I turned toward the sound of it. It was several shocked moments before I realized what I was looking at. *Who* I was looking at.

"Die, wish."

"Jonathan?" I gasped.

His face was completely deformed, his forehead sloping back, his nose and mouth elongated like a muzzle. His few remaining teeth were long and pointed, his gums bleeding profusely.

His body was in a similar, half-formed state, with long, gangly arms and legs bent awkwardly like a dog's haunches. He was naked, half covered in fur and half in rotting flesh.

He looked like a shifter caught mid-shift, and now he pointed a gnarled, twisted finger at me.

"Die, wish."

Witch. That's what he'd been saying. *Die, witch.*

"What the fuck *are* you?" I unsheathed the dagger and got to my feet, but disgust and astonishment—and a flicker of pity—made me hesitate. Was he in pain? Could he move? How had he even reached the summit?

What the hell had he done to himself?

He was pitifully broken, blood dripping onto the snow where he stood. A soft whimper escaped his lips.

And then he lunged.

Despite appearances, he was faster and stronger than a human. Stronger than me. He barreled into me at full speed —shifter speed—knocking me to the ground easily.

The beast was on top of me, pinning me in the snow, my arms trapped uselessly beneath his weight. I clung to Sophie's dagger, but it didn't do me any good. I couldn't move.

Jonathan snapped his teeth in front of my face, spattering blood across my cheeks. It was a show of dominance more than a real threat, and I wondered how long he'd drag this out. How long he'd torture me.

He'd spent his entire adult life doing just that.

Rage bubbled inside, and a flicker of my magic stirred to life.

"You're pathetic!" I shouted, squirming beneath his weight. Inside, my blood warmed, the magic humming through my veins. Gathering strength. "Look what you've done to yourself. You couldn't hack it as a man, and now you're just a freak. An abomination."

"Not abomination. Choice," he slurred. "My choice."

"You didn't choose this. No one would choose this. You tried to make yourself into something you aren't—something better. And you failed, Jonathan. Everything you've ever done has failed."

He swung his monstrous head from side to side, as if to tell me no.

Then, he howled. Gasped. Sputtered.

And I stared in horror as the bones beneath his face shifted, his body slowly returning to its damaged human form. The weight on my chest lifted.

I could breathe again.

I could move my arms.

"I wanted this," he said, his words clarifying. "It was the only way I could—"

I slammed the dagger into his side, shoving his dead weight off my body.

Jonathan gasped, and I rolled on top of him, pinning

him down. Blood leaked from the wound, staining the snow ruby red.

"It was your father's way," I said, my hands igniting with blue fire.

Take it. Take it. Take it.

The magic whispered inside me, hungry for his soul. I wondered if I'd rip it out of his throat again. If he even *had* his soul anymore.

"It's *always* been his," I said. I wanted him to know this. Wanted it to be the last thing he heard. "Nothing you've ever done has been yours, and now you're going to die knowing you lived your entire life as a shadow puppet."

Gasping for air beneath me, Jonathan almost looked human. Almost regretful.

"Gray, I'm…" He stilled, his green grass eyes holding mine. He seemed to be searching for his words, and for a brief second, I actually thought he might apologize for all the things he'd done to me. To my mother. To Sophie. To everyone who wasn't his father's idea of perfect.

But that's not how the world worked. Not everyone changed. Not everyone redeemed himself in the end.

I yanked the dagger from his side and pressed the tip to his throat. Magic swirled around the blade.

Cut his throat. Make it slow. Make him hurt.

For so long, I'd wanted to torture him. Make him pay for what he'd done to my family and friends. What he'd been doing for ten years.

But now, I just wanted it to be done.

"You know why I have to do this," I whispered, an

unexpected knot of emotion tightening my throat. "I'm sorry it had to be this way. I'm sorry for what you've been through. I hope you find peace."

"I'm *not* sorry," he continued, his eyes blazing with new fire. "My father and uncles were right. Witches need to be eradicated. It's the only way the rightful—"

I shoved the dagger through his throat.

In the end, I hadn't needed magic to do it. Just will.

I got to my feet, waiting for his soul to slither out for the last time.

But there was only the white fog of his breath, thinning into nothing.

Jonathan Reese was dead.

I thought the moment would feel bigger somehow. More important. The closing of an epic story my life had been writing for a long, long time.

But it was just a moment, not so different from any other. Here, and then gone.

The air before me stirred, and a massive snowy owl appeared—one of Liam's messengers. He was white with black spots and an all-white face, his piercing amber eyes looking right through me, pinning me in place.

He hovered over Jonathan's body, watching me. Waiting.

He was magnificent. The sight of him brought tears to my eyes. I reached out to touch him, but in a swirl of snow and ice, he vanished.

I blinked the cold from my eyes. When I glanced down at the spot where Jonathan's body had lain, all that remained was Sophie's dagger, glistening in the bright red snow.

I crouched down to pick it up, but as soon as I touched it, the ground began to rumble.

Another earthquake?

I fell to my knees as a fissure split the snow, the sound like the most terrifying crack of thunder I'd ever heard.

And then the mountain crumbled.

Not an earthquake, I realized. *An avalanche.*

I sucked in a breath of icy air as the solid ground dropped out from under me. The world spun and blurred into white nothingness, and I tumbled backward, wind whipping my hair and stealing my breath, ice and snow slicing my skin. I squeezed my eyes shut as the sound of a thousand freight trains descended on me, and then I was flying.

Through the snow, through the air, through solid ice, I could no longer tell. I only knew that when I finally reached the bottom, no one would be there to catch my fall.

TWENTY-THREE

GRAY

"Gray. Can you hear me?"

The whispers tickled the back of my mind, slowly drifting into my consciousness.

"Gray?"

Gray. That was my name, but why was that voice so far away? A million miles, at least.

Where was I?

Falling.

I couldn't open my eyes. Couldn't feel my body.

Mountain.

The wind howled like a banshee, carrying with it the rest of my memories.

Avalanche.

Images slammed into my mind, one after the other. The snow. The ice. The terrible rumbling. The fall.

Had it broken my neck? My back?

I gave myself a moment to breathe. To be still.

The wind faded.

All was silent again. I wondered if the snowy owl would come for me.

I wondered if I would leave a ruby-red stain in the snow like Jonathan had.

I wondered if Liam would ever find me. I wanted to thank him for our time on the beach. For all he'd done for me. For being him.

"Gray, I need you to open your eyes."

Another whisper, and the scent of something I used to know.

"Gray, can you hear me? Please open your eyes."

More whispers, louder now. Clearer. The heady smell of expensive whiskey and soft leather.

I know that voice. I know that smell…

"Stay with me, love."

Darius?

My eyelids fluttered open, and slowly—agonizingly— the picture came into focus. A beautiful dark-haired man was looking down at me through warm golden eyes, his full lips pressed together in worry.

It smelled like my vampire. Looked like him. *Felt* like him, my blood already warming in response to his presence.

"Darius?" I whispered.

A smile broke across his concerned face. "Yes. I'm here, love. I've got you."

It was too good to be true. Another trick of the realm. Another torment.

"You're not real," I whispered, torn between wanting the words to be false and wishing the torment of these nightmares would just end. I had to stay focused. Strong. The gateway to my own realm—that was my mission. I had to keep following the pull in my gut to that place—the place that would lead me home. There wasn't room for fear.

"I'll try not to take that as an insult, love. But only because you've been through quite an ordeal. As soon as you've fully recovered, I'll be waiting for a proper apology."

The accent was perfect—it definitely sounded like Darius.

I told my arms to move, told my hands to reach up and touch his face, but they wouldn't obey.

"You're in bad shape, Gray. I need to get you inside."

"Okay."

"I'm afraid this is going to hurt," he whispered, pressing a soft kiss to my temple. "Whatever you do, don't let go."

"I won't. Ever."

His arms tightened around me, and he hefted me up out of the snow. The movement sent a shockwave of pain rippling throughout my body, so intense it threatened to suck me under.

I tried to hold on. Tried to stay conscious. Tried to concentrate on the feel of the strong, capable arms of my vampire, wrapped tightly around my body, carrying me someplace warm and safe.

I even tried to smile.

But then the world began to spin again, and in its utter cruelty, sucked me away into nothingness.

TWENTY-FOUR

GRAY

Soft orange light flickered against my eyelids, the hiss and pop of a roaring fire stirring me from a deep sleep.

I opened my eyes and took in my new surroundings—a cozy, one-room cabin in the middle of a snowy wood. Outside, harsh winter wind howled through the pines and blew snow into a white frenzy, but inside I was warm and safe, tucked into a small bed beside the fire. I'd been bathed and dressed in a soft, clean T-shirt that fell to my knees, my wounds not only treated, but healed.

Sophie's dagger rested on the hearth above the fireplace. I couldn't believe I'd held onto it.

"Feeling better, love?" Darius knelt by my side and took my hand, pressing a kiss to my fingers. His golden eyes shone with relief.

"You're... you're really here." I sat up in bed, astonished. "I thought maybe I was hallucinating."

215

"Not about this." His voice was like warm honey. "Are you in any pain?"

I wriggled my toes and took a deep breath, assessing. I felt strong. I felt... amazing.

"I'm... really great, actually." I squeezed his hand, bringing it to my chest and holding it there. "What happened at the portal? Is Ronan here, too?"

"Not yet, but he will be. I came through first. Liam was waiting for me on arrival, and directed me to you. From the looks of it, I got here just in time."

I nodded. I didn't know what would've happened if he hadn't found me. Would the owl have come? Would I have awoken in some other strange landscape, fighting yet another enemy?

"Liam is awaiting word about Ronan," Darius continued. "As soon as he hears anything, he'll let us know, and we'll figure out where to meet up."

I nodded and leaned back against the pillow. Darius brushed the hair from my forehead, his fingers tracing soft swirls on my skin.

"How did you find this place?" I asked.

"It simply appeared, right when we most needed it."

"The realm is like that. It seems to give us what we need. Sometimes that also happens to be what we want, but not always." I shrugged, snuggling deeper into the heavenly bed. "We got lucky this time."

I told him about what had happened on the summit. About Jonathan, and then the avalanche.

"You were hypothermic when I found you," he said, the

words making him wince. "You'd suffered several broken bones and fractures, and frostbite covering half of your body. Internal bleeding was another concern. I thought..." Darius closed his eyes and shook his head.

I heard the words anyway.

I thought I'd lost you.

"How did you heal me?" I asked him.

"Unfortunately, *El Lobo* was not here to make his chicken soup. So I had to settle for the next best thing." He tapped his wrist.

Vampire blood.

"It didn't require much. Our blood bond is strong, Gray. You respond to my blood in a way I've never seen in other bonded—" He cut himself off, flustered. "Well, in any case, it seems to have done the trick."

What had he meant to say? Bonded pairs? Bonded mates?

I didn't know much about vampire society, or how things like mates actually worked. I knew it was an intense commitment. Knew that a vampire would die before he let harm come to his mate. And I knew that while vampires might experience many partnerships and, frankly, sexual encounters, he only mated once in his entire immortal life.

When we'd first made the blood bond, I'd assumed it was more transactional—a legal and binding contract.

But now?

Mates? Was that what we were becoming? Is that how he saw me?

The idea sent a little thrill down my spine.

"Thank you," I whispered. "For saving me." My hand trailed up his arm to his face, my fingers brushing across his lips, his jaw, taking him in one slow, deliberate touch at a time.

His golden eyes sparkled.

"Hello, little brawler," he whispered, brushing his lips across my brow. His whiskey-and-leather scent washed over me in a soothing wave.

"So it's... really you?" I whispered. "This isn't a hallucination?"

"It's really me," he said, lowering his mouth to mine.

The hot press of his lips was familiar, yet overwhelming, like the first sip of water after a lifetime of thirst. I tasted him slowly, terrified that the moment I let my guard down, the realm would shift and he'd morph into another monster, or burst into flames before my eyes, or liquify into a pool of blood in my mouth.

But none of those things came to pass. There was only Darius, his kiss growing more insistent, his tongue sweeping into my mouth, his touch light as he slid a hand beneath my shirt.

I let out a soft moan.

He paused, breaking our kiss. "Are you sure you're feeling okay?"

"I'm sure. Better than ever."

Darius resumed our kiss and cupped my breast, thumb grazing my nipple, the barest touch sending a pulse of heat to my core.

I sighed in his mouth, and he deepened our kiss, his

touch growing more possessive as he slid his fingers down the front of my underwear. I was already wet for him, arching to get closer.

"Do I feel real enough yet, love?" he teased, nipping my bottom lip as his fingers slowly sank inside me, his thumb ghosting over my clit. "Because this," he breathed, dragging his fingers all the way out, then thrusting them back in, hitting me *just* right. "This feels *very* real to me. And very hot. And very, *very* wet."

My core throbbed, pulsing with need and desire as his fingers slid in and out, teasing me into a white-hot frenzy.

I grabbed his arm, digging my nails into his flesh. He was no longer that first sip of water, but the very last—a drink I desperately needed to consume before it disappeared forever.

"Real," I panted. "Definitely real."

"Are you sure? Perhaps you're still hallucinating."

"I don't care if I'm hallucinating. Just don't stop touching me."

"That is an order with which I'll happily comply." He kissed my jaw, my neck, swirling his tongue in the hollow of my throat before kissing his way down the front of my chest.

He sucked my nipple through the shirt, biting gently. The extra layer between his mouth and my flesh made the teasing all the more exquisite, and my hips rocked forward, urging his fingers deeper inside me.

"Your scent is..." He inhaled deeply, closing his eyes.

"Overpowering me. I can't... I... Bloody hell, woman. I need to taste you."

"Anything," I breathed.

Up to that point, he'd still been kneeling at my side, but now he climbed into the bed on top of me, kissing his way down my stomach, across the tops of each thigh, and inside each knee as he slid my underwear off and parted my legs. With a soft, seductive sigh, he lowered his head, flicking his tongue against my clit.

His silky hair brushed my skin, and I held my breath in anticipation, my thighs already trembling for him.

"More," I breathed.

He licked a slow, teasing path up my center, sucking my clit between his teeth, and my whole body melted into the sheets like butter in a pan.

Between my thighs, I felt my vampire shudder.

"Darius," I panted. "That's... yes. Right there. I can't..."

Darius groaned, searing my flesh with his insistent mouth. There were no more teasing touches, no more soft, slow swirls of pleasure. Suddenly I was being *devoured*.

His hands gripped my thighs and pinned them to the bed, and he fucked me with his tongue, his lips, his breath, all of it pushing me to the very edge of my limits, the edge of my sanity. The cabin walls spun around me, and I arched my hips off the bed, squirming beneath him, almost unable to take another minute of his hot, insistent mouth.

He overpowered me easily, tightening his grip on my thighs, shoving his tongue deep inside me in one last, powerful thrust, unleashing an explosive orgasm that rocked my core. There was no warning, no slow build. Only ecstasy. I fisted his hair and pulled him closer, rocking against his mouth, riding out the very last ripples of pure pleasure.

Before my muscles had even stopped trembling, Darius shifted between my legs, guiding them over his shoulders, pushing against the backs of my thighs as he leaned in for another kiss, my taste fresh on his lips. His rock-hard cock brushed my clit, unleashing another aftershock of pleasure that made me shiver.

He pulled back from our kiss and looked deep into my eyes, his own eyes dark with desire and lust and something else—something that made my heart beat faster and my stomach tremble. Something that went beyond mates and blood bonds.

Something I was afraid to name, because if I said it out loud, it might just disappear.

"You absolutely intoxicate me," he whispered.

I couldn't speak, so I only smiled, arching up against his cock, letting my body tell him *exactly* what kind of effect he was having on me.

Intoxicating didn't even begin to cover it.

Darius moaned softly, but he didn't break his gaze, refusing to sever the connection that seemed to be holding us both together. Here. Now.

Real.

Sliding a hand under my ass, he rolled his hips, plunging that perfect length deep inside me. I gasped in pleasure, and he captured my mouth in another searing kiss, fucking me deeper, harder, making me more delirious with every thrust.

I was coming unglued, even as his kisses held me together. I tried to fight it, tried to hold on a little bit longer, tried to savor it. But he was too perfect, too wild, too intense, and in the end, I had no choice but to let go.

With a final cry of pure ecstasy, I tumbled over the edge, falling and falling and falling, my body tightening around him as he fucked me harder and faster, both of us clinging to each other as our two hot, glistening bodies shattered into a million pieces.

When I finally caught my breath again, I opened my eyes to find I was still in Darius's arms, still whole and alive.

I smiled, my eyes blurring with tears.

Somehow, he'd found a way to put my pieces back together.

TWENTY-FIVE

DARIUS

"You know, *vampire*," Gray said, turning over in my arms so her backside fit snugly against my front. We'd spent the last hour devouring each other without words, but I could tell from the teasing tone in her voice that I was quickly heading for a battle of wills.

"Just say it, little brawler."

"I was just thinking about our deal, and all of our conversations since then, and I seem to recall something about pre-conditions."

Biting back a smile, I said, "I'm certain I don't know what you're talking about."

"No? You don't remember that whole 'in my bed, I'm in charge, and you will beg me for it' thing?"

"My memory is... not what it used to be."

"This certainly doesn't *feel* like your bedroom," she went on, ignoring me.

I smiled into her hair, inhaling her sweet scent. "No, it doesn't."

"And I don't recall having to beg you for it."

"No, you certainly didn't."

"Interesting, D. I really thought you'd stick to your guns on this one. Are you really that much of a pushover that you'd let one little witch take advantage of you?"

"We're in the Shadowrealm," I reminded her. "Technically, it doesn't count."

"Ah, I see. The old 'what happens in the Shadowrealm stays in the Shadowrealm' defense."

"Indeed."

"So you're saying you want to take it all back?"

"What I'm saying, little brawler..." I nipped the back of her neck, making her squeal. "...is the moment we get back home, all the old rules apply. I will take you in my bed, and you *will* beg me for it."

She wriggled against me, the touch of her soft, warm flesh making me hard as steel. "Ha! I think we both know who'll be doing the begging in this arrangement."

"You win," I said, knowing full well she was right. Now that I'd tasted her, filled her, there was nothing I wouldn't give her, nothing I wouldn't do to hear the hum of pleasure in her blood as she screamed my name.

I pressed another kiss to the back of her neck, then reluctantly crawled out of bed. The temperature outside had dropped to below freezing, and I worried she'd grow cold again.

After seeing her in the snow like that, bent and broken,

so pale she was nearly blue... I never wanted her to be cold again.

I placed a few more logs on the fire, stoking it back to a crackling roar.

When I returned to our bed, she was staring up at the ceiling, her face contemplative.

I crawled back in beside her and pulled her against my chest like before, her back to me. I liked her this way, safe and protected in my arms. "What are you thinking about, love?"

"Our blood bond," she said, her voice made even softer by the crackling fire before us.

"What of it?"

"Does it connect our memories, somehow?"

I considered her question. "I suppose it's possible. It allows me to sense you and your magic, so it stands to reason it might allow you to sense certain things about me as well. Why do you ask?"

"You said you healed me with some of your blood."

"Yes, but it was a very small amount. Nothing that would harm you."

"I remember tasting it now," she said. "The richness on my tongue. It wasn't like Jonathan's. It was... soothing. I felt it sort of... I don't know. Like I wasn't actually swallowing it, but letting it sink into me, deep down. Immediately after that, I drifted into this strange dream... But now I'm thinking maybe it wasn't a dream at all."

"Tell me," I said.

"It was a long time ago, back when people still had

horses and carriages instead of cars. I was in London, and I thought I saw…" She trailed off, almost as if she were afraid to say it out loud. Afraid she'd seen a ghost.

In many ways, I believed she had.

"What did you see, love?" I asked gently, though I already suspected her answer. There was only one reason she'd be dreaming of my home city, my home century.

"Your… your family," she said, each word laden with pain. Hers, mine, that of my children… What did it matter now? I was so tangled up in her, so deeply connected to her that her pain felt like mine, mine like hers.

I'd been thinking of them when I'd healed her. How could I not? The threat of actually losing Gray stirred a deep sense of fear and loss inside me, reminding me of so many other losses in my life. My human life.

Somehow, I'd transferred those memories to her.

"There was a woman," she continued. "With gorgeous curly black hair and olive-green eyes."

I pressed a kiss to her bare shoulder, pulling her closer to my chest. "My wife, Emmaline," I said. It'd been a long time since I'd said her name out loud, but it still hurt just the same. "We had two children—Devin and Katarina."

"I saw them, too. Your daughter had hair like her mom, right?"

"Oh, yes." I laughed, the memory bittersweet. "Emmaline loved her curls, but Katarina hated them. She begged us to cut her hair short like her brother's. Said her curls always got tangled in tree branches, preventing her from climbing as quickly as the boys. Emmaline spent more time pulling leaves and sticks out of Kat's hair than she spent bandaging Devin's skinned knees."

Gray let out a soft laugh, the sound of it as bittersweet as mine had been. "Your family was beautiful, Darius."

"Yes," I said, because it was true. They *were* beautiful. Loving. Happy. They'd been the joys of my life. I had been blessed.

"Do you still think of them?" she asked.

"It was a long time ago, Gray."

"Darius," she breathed, and I could tell from the deep note of sadness in her voice that she'd finally decided to ask me the inevitable question. Rolling onto her back and gazing up into my eyes, she said, "How were you turned?"

I traced my thumb across her lips. If we were to share memories, I would've much rather she'd seen my family, the precious time that I'd been given with them. I would've wanted her to hear my children's laughter, smell the apple cakes my wife baked for our birthdays. But when it came to the story of my past, I couldn't cherry-pick the highlights. This, too, was part of that story. Part of my very creation. It was ugly and terrible, but it had happened. I could no more change it than I could snap my fingers and take us out of this realm.

"It is not a pretty story, Gray."

"I know." Her cheeks darkened, and she lowered her eyes. "I'm sorry. You don't have to tell me. I... I didn't mean to pry. I just—"

"It's not that. It's..." I traced my thumb across her lips

again, and she looked up at me once more, catching me as always in her soothing, blue-eyed gaze.

Something in my chest tightened—a warning that had been lingering in my heart from the moment Gray and I had connected at Black Ruby. From the moment I'd sealed our blood bond.

Learning someone's deepest, darkest secrets carried inevitable consequences. Gray would never look at me the same after this. Where now there was passion and friendship and desire and trust and maybe even love, as soon as I said the words of this tale, there would be pity. It would recolor everything she knew about me, everything she saw in me.

I supposed I could've made it easy on myself—on both of us—and fabricated a more comfortable explanation. That I would've died without turning, perhaps. Or that becoming a vampire had been my choice.

But the feelings I had for Gray were real, growing deeper every moment I spent with her. And a love built on deception, no matter how pure the intention, was no better than a paper boat set upon a stormy sea. It might float for a time, but in the end, it would only disintegrate.

"A year prior to my turning," I began, "my younger brother Marcus disappeared. He'd always had a touch of wanderlust in his blood, like our father before us, so initially we'd thought he'd stowed away on a merchant ship to America, or taken a train to Eastern Europe. He'd done that sort of thing before, and had always turned up back in London after a time, with a happy glint in his eyes and plenty of stories to tell. But this time, weeks stretched into months, and after four months without word, we began to worry. We sent messages to his associates far and wide, contacted the police, did everything we could to try to track him down."

"Did you hear back from anyone?" she asked.

"No one had any information. We feared he'd gotten into trouble with the law in a foreign country and was imprisoned, or that he'd been injured or incapacitated with no way of reaching us. Eventually, we mourned him as dead."

The fire hissed, shooting sparks into the chimney. I watched its orange light dance on the wall beside the bed. Gray remained silent.

"Exactly one year and a day since his disappearance," I continued, "I returned home from my office in the city to find Marcus sitting in my gardens, dressed in fine silks and looking for all the world like an aristocrat. He was still Marcus, of course, but it seemed as though someone had erased all the flaws and imperfections that had made him human. He had no wrinkles, none of the cares that he used to wear like a heavy coat over his shoulders. And his eyes, once a deep brown, had lightened to a warm gold that caught and held the light in a way I knew couldn't be natural."

"Like yours," she said, her hand warm against my cheek.

I nodded, kissing her palm.

"I'd heard stories about vampires," I said, "but until that

moment, I'd never considered them real. Then Marcus smiled at me, his teeth glinting in the moonlight, and said, 'Do you know what I am, brother?' And I found myself nodding, even though my mind was railing against the very thought of it. I was holding out for a sane explanation, a punchline on a year-long joke my brother had most certainly played on us."

I closed my eyes, not wanting to see the change in her eyes that would inevitably come from hearing these words. This confession.

"My brother offered to turn me," I said plainly, recalling that moment as if it were yesterday. "When I refused, he overpowered me and did it anyway."

Gray's gasp sent a pang into my heart. "But... why? Why would your own brother do something like that?"

"I spent a lot of time thinking about that, looking for some deep, complex explanation that would allow me to understand and—ultimately—forgive him. Perhaps he was coerced, I'd thought. Or maybe he truly believed he was offering me a precious gift, that my life would be so much better once I'd made the change." I swallowed through the tightness in my throat, shocked that even after so many centuries, I still couldn't accept the fact that he'd actually done it. "But in the end, I kept coming back to the truth as he'd confessed it the very next day: Marcus simply couldn't bear the thought of living an eternity alone."

"Did you kill him?" she whispered. "Once you were strong enough?"

"Oh, I thought of it, certainly. But I knew that wouldn't

change my fate. Wouldn't return my life to me, wouldn't return my family. In those early days, the bloodlust was terrifying; I didn't trust myself not to hurt Emmaline and the children, so I implored my brother to help me fake my own death in an accident, knowing it would bring them more peace that way. An accident was a horrible thing, but a real one, not a fairytale. They would grieve, they would struggle, but they wouldn't lose their minds. Ultimately, they might find peace again. Maybe even happiness."

Gray was silent for so long, I wondered if she'd fallen asleep. But then she shifted onto her hip and took my face in her hands, waiting patiently until I finally met her gaze again.

Her eyes shone with emotion. Not with pity, but sympathy. Empathy. She, too, had lost someone she loved to a person she thought she could trust. She, too, had had her choices taken away, her life's trajectory altered as a result.

She understood this pain. I didn't know why I'd ever feared she wouldn't.

It was a strange thing, connecting with someone so deeply over such betrayal, such loss. There was a certain comfort in knowing you weren't alone, but that knowledge was a double-edged sword. It meant that someone you loved had also endured the kind of pain that had nearly destroyed you. The kind of pain you'd give your own life to spare them from.

I brushed a curl from her forehead, tucking it behind her ear, staring at her in wonderment. How had fate seen fit to bring this woman into my life? To crack open the heart I'd sealed off centuries ago?

"And Marcus?" she asked softly. "Where is he now?"

"Several weeks after turning me, he was traveling in Scotland, where he inadvertently crossed paths with a local vampire hunter. He was beheaded. Quite painlessly, from what I was told."

"So he turned you just so he wouldn't have to face immortality by himself, and then he got himself killed a few weeks later?"

"A cruel twist of irony," I said. "Soon after, I relocated to America. I didn't want to be reminded of my family. I knew eventually my wife would remarry, and my children would grow and have children of their own—that's what I wanted for them. Eventually, they, too, would die, and so would their children, and all of the children who'd come after. Yet I would linger endlessly, forced to watch their lives begin and end from a distance, like a stranger trapped outside with his faced pressed to the glass."

A tear slipped down her cheek.

"I don't know what to say, Darius. I... I hate that you had to go through that. You lost your family. Your life. All because of someone who should've loved you enough to spare you that fate."

"Love is funny that way, isn't it? You think it comes with all these guarantees, all these failsafes—especially with family. With blood. But in reality, 'should' has nothing to do with it."

Gray frowned, the faint line between her eyes deepening. "I'm sorry," she whispered. "For all of it."

"It brought me to you, Gray. How could I possibly wish for another outcome?"

"You're saying that *now*, but if you'd never met me—"

"If I'd never met you," I said, cupping her face and stroking her cheeks with my thumbs, "the world would be a pale imitation, the monotony of which I'd wander through like a ghost."

"But—"

I captured her mouth in a bruising kiss, swallowing her words before she could voice any more protests. She yielded easily, melting softly in my arms.

I rolled on top of her, cradling her head as she parted her legs and invited me inside her once again. It was an effort to hold back, to stay present, to not explode the moment her soft, warm flesh enveloped me. I had never felt anything so perfect, so exquisite as this woman. Her warmth called to me, and as I slid deeper inside, my eyes closed in ecstasy, in wonder, in gratitude, and I thought of home.

For so many years, it had been a place—a memory of a past that no longer existed, a collection of ghosts I'd clung to because I didn't know how to set them free.

But now, *home* was simply a feeling, big and immense and powerful, all of it wrapped up in this woman in my arms. I could no longer separate the two—I no longer wanted to. *She* was my home. My heart.

I kissed her fiercely, worshipping her flesh, her lips, her

breasts. I slid out from between her thighs and kissed my way down her belly, tasting her soft heat again, savoring her moans as I coaxed them from her body one blissful, earth-shattering orgasm at a time.

I don't know how long we carried on, losing ourselves in that pleasure, that heat. Only that it was nearly dawn when I awoke from a dreamless sleep, realizing we'd both drifted off at some point in the night.

I was already hard for her again, and about to rouse her for one more kiss, one more moment of bliss, when I sensed a visitor lingering outside the cabin, too nervous to knock on the door.

Not bothering to dress, I crept from the bed and opened the door, leaning against the threshold. Our guest's eyes widened as his gaze trailed down to my cock, and I laughed heartily.

It wasn't every day a vampire could catch Death off guard.

TWENTY-SIX

GRAY

A chilly breeze drifted in from the front of the cabin, stirring me awake.

Darius stood in the doorway laughing, his bare backside tempting in the soft glow of the fire's remaining embers.

"Here to join us, Mr. Colebrook?" Darius teased. "If so, I suggest you consider alternate clothing options."

Mr. Colebrook?

"Liam!" I bolted up in bed, a smile stretched across my face.

Liam cleared his throat. "I am here to… I was… I'm simply… Yes. I'm very sorry for the intrusion, as I can see you're quite occupied."

"Occupied," Darius said, his tone still teasing. He was enjoying this.

"Busy," Liam stammered. "Very busy. I must speak with you both, rather urgently, but perhaps I'll just give you a moment to—"

235

"Welcome back, Liam." I stood beside Darius in the doorway, the bed sheet wrapped around my body, my sex-hair a wild mess, and grinned.

"Gray!" His eyes lit up when he saw me, then darkened with the same desirous haze I'd seen on the beach. "You're looking... well."

He was blushing again, but I probably was, too. Thoughts of our day on the beach flooded my mind, and a tiny electric current raced down my spine.

"Your heart rate has gone a bit erratic, love," Darius said, touching the back of my neck. "And your blood is..." Darius inhaled deeply, then looked at me, back to Liam, and back to me again.

His full lips parted in a broad, all-knowing smirk. "Well now. This *is* an interesting development. Would either of you care to elaborate?"

Liam remained silent. I bit my lip and shook my head, trying not to smile.

Darius quirked an eyebrow at my silence, but that only made me laugh.

"What happens in the realm stays in the realm, right, D?"

Liam cleared his throat again, still slightly flustered. "If you wouldn't mind putting on pants, vampire..."

"Well, *I* wouldn't mind," Darius said, "But Gray might. She prefers me pantless. Don't you, love?" He folded his arms across his chest, his eyes sparkling with laughter.

I cracked up that. He had a point.

I looked between the two men—my vampire and my...

well, my Liam—my heart warm and full. Darius and I had gotten so much closer since that first night at Black Ruby, and though I'd only gotten a glimpse at Liam's bottomless depths, I sensed it was the beginning of something very special between us. Between *all* of us. Liam, Darius, Ronan, Asher, Emilio... we were meant to be in one another's lives. In so many ways, it felt like we always had been.

"Are you alright, love?" Darius asked, his smile softening.

I blinked away the tears that'd glazed my eyes and nodded. All of these feelings, this emotion, this intensity... maybe it should've been difficult to navigate, but it wasn't.

It felt natural and whole and immensely beautiful. But it was also still so very new, and I was afraid that if I tried to talk about my feelings too soon, or put a label on anything, it would shatter.

"So I take it you've found our demon," Darius said, stepping out onto the porch, still pantsless. "Ronan!" he called out into the snowy dawn. The sun here wouldn't harm him. It wasn't earth's sun. Technically, it wasn't even real. "Come in and sit by the fire. Gray has worn me out completely—you must take her off my hands."

"He's not here," Liam said.

"What?" I gasped. "Where is he?"

"I've received word from one of my ravens. He's just arrived in the realm, not far from the Pool of Unknowing."

"The Pool of Unknowing?" A bolt of awareness shot into my mind, and I closed my eyes as the vision formed—a deep, still pool that looked like the night sky, with swirls of dark violet and blue, dotted with bright, glittering stars. A ring of smooth gray rocks surrounded it, each one as ancient as time itself. Lotus blossoms floated in a cluster in the center.

And there, just beneath the water's calm surface, was the rune gate—my stone archway, glowing with bright blue runes, lighting the pathway back to my realm. Back home.

"That's where we're supposed to go," I said, never more certain than I'd been in that moment. "That's where the gateway will be."

TWENTY-SEVEN

EMILIO

Talia was tall and thin, with shoulder-length hair the color of dark red wine and skin that glowed in the moonlight.

She was also two hours late.

I made a show of glancing at my phone, but she ignored it, taking a seat across from me at a table in the abandoned Hannaford Distillery tasting room. They used to do tours and events here, but the place went bottom up years ago. Now it was just another abandoned storefront, perfect for clandestine meetings and shady dealings.

"I trust we're alone here?" she asked, glancing around the dark room. The only light came from the moon, shining in through the blown-out windows.

She hadn't specified whether she meant here in the tasting room or here in the general vicinity, so I nodded. She didn't need to know that Lansky and Hobb were keeping their eyes on me from an abandoned glass factory across the street.

I was fairly certain she had her own backup hidden in the shadows.

"Have you uncovered anything further to back up your claims?" she asked, her pale gold eyes even more devious in the darkness.

"We've got people following up on the information from our source, but so far, they haven't turned up anything." My sister's team had combed the beach, searching every pier and boat launch they could find. They'd even contacted a local geologist, but as far as he knew, none of the rocky cliffs contained cave systems.

"Who exactly is this source?" Talia asked.

"I'm not at liberty to—"

"Don't play games with me, Detective. This is a very delicate situation. I'm sure you can appreciate the need for thoroughness."

"As I'm sure you can appreciate the need for discretion."

We glared at each other across the table, neither willing to back down. Talia scared the shit out of me, especially in person, but something was different about her this time.

She was scared, too.

"This is big, Talia. Bigger than Raven's Cape. Bigger than a few hunters terrorizing a community of witches."

Talia said nothing.

I slammed my fist on the table, but she didn't even flinch.

"What aren't you telling me?" I snapped.

She stared down at my fist for a long time before speaking again, and when she did, her voice was quiet.

Almost... reverent.

"The power in our communities is shifting, Detective. Weakening. Can you not feel it?"

"What I feel is an imbalance left by the witches and other beings who were murdered and stolen from their homes."

She looked up at me, her eyes dancing with new light. Excitement. "Then we agree that witches are to blame?"

"They're not to blame, Talia. They didn't kill themselves."

"They've allowed themselves to become weak and complacent. Is that not the same thing?"

"How can you say that? Listen to yourself!" I shoved back my chair, unable to sit still. I couldn't believe the bullshit she was spewing. I knew the Council was hands-off and out of touch with the day-to-day realities of most supernatural communities. But to say that witches had brought this on themselves? It was the kind of absolutely backward thinking that had led to the witch trials and hunts of old, and there was no place for it. Not with me. Not anywhere.

"There's no need to get upset," she said. "I'm simply stating the facts. As a detective, I thought you'd appreciate that."

"You're stating regurgitated nonsense that should've died out in the stone age. Witches are the chosen guardians of earth's magic. They should be revered, not hunted and vilified."

"There are some who believe they never should've been entrusted with magic in the first place."

"Some who believe? Jesus, Talia. Are you working for the hunters now?"

Talia smoothed an elegant hand over her wine-colored hair, as though my simmering anger had somehow ruffled her appearance.

When she looked at me again, her eyes glittered with so much malice, it was an effort to keep my predatory instincts in check—to stay in human form.

"The hunters' methods may be primitive and cruel," she said, "but those methods stem from a deep sense of right and wrong, and a loyalty to truth and righteousness."

"Unbelievable. Do you realize—"

"The *witches*," she continued, "are a problem that should've been dealt with long ago, and for that, I take some responsibility. The Council has not been as involved as we should've been. That is changing." She shook her head, her lips twisting into a smarmy smile. "Oh, don't give me that look, Detective. I'm not suggesting they be burned at the stake. Merely that we work together to find a way to make the distribution of power more equitable."

My jaw popped, my muscles rippling beneath the skin. My wolf wanted out. He wanted to tear out her throat.

I headed for the window, taking in a breath of cool air.

When I returned to the table, Talia's smile was gone.

"I want to help you, Detective Alvarez. But in order to

do so, I need you to trust me. I need you to share with me any pertinent information you have about this case."

"You want some information?" I practically growled at her. "Fine. Let's start with this one: Orendiel. Ring any bells?"

Her already pale face turned absolutely translucent, her mouth parting in a state of surprise I was pretty damn sure she hadn't meant to show.

"Darkwinter," I continued. "I don't know how or why, but they've teamed up with the hunters. Right now they seem to be targeting witches, along with shifters and vampires in slightly smaller numbers. But I'm not telling you anything you don't already know, am I?"

Her stunned silence was all the confirmation I needed.

How long had she been sitting on this? Was she covering up for the fact that the Council had let this situation get so out of control right under their very noses? Was she embarrassed? Worried about political fallout?

Or worse—actually involved in this?

Leaning across the table, I lowered my face to hers, staring into her golden eyes as my breath stirred her perfect hair. "Once Darkwinter helps the hunters eradicate the witches, who do you think they'll aim for next? You think they'll pack up their toys and go back to their own sand-box? Or do you think they've got bigger aspirations? The Council, perhaps? The Courts?"

"Careful, wolf," she hissed, but I'd rattled her. I could see it in the slight inward curve of her shoulders. She seemed to be shrinking from me.

"I'm pointing out the obvious here, Talia. Shifters are much less a threat to hunters. Our power lies in our ability to take on animal forms—to embody their strengths and instincts. It makes *us* stronger. But fae magic? *Your* magic? It makes *them* weaker. Once they figure that out, it won't be long before they're knocking down the doors of your precious ivory tower. And when that day comes, I hope to *hell* you don't come down here looking for help."

Despite her obvious fear, the ice in her eyes told me that I'd just crossed into uncharted territory. It'd taken decades to forge a decent working relationship with the Council, and it damn near killed me to see it all unraveling. But I couldn't stand by and let her get away with this. There were lives at stake—lives of people I cared about.

And that was just the beginning.

"Despite our differences," she said, rising from her chair like a tree growing from a rock, "there is one thing we've got in common, wolf."

"Yeah? What's that?"

She leaned in close, her lips brushing the shell of my ear.

"Survival instinct," she whispered. When she pulled back, her smile was menacing, cutting through all pretense of professionalism like a hot knife. "Enjoy the rest of your stay in Raven's Cape, Detective. Good night."

TWENTY-EIGHT

GRAY

"It's here," I said, my heartbeat quickening as the pool's stone perimeter came into view. "I can feel it. It's like it's calling to me, and my magic is calling back."

Darius, Liam, and I had been hiking for hours, and we'd just crested a hill, giving us a glimpse of the Pool of Unknowing and the dark green valley that stretched out below. We'd left the snows behind at the cabin, and now the air was balmy and sweet, buzzing with insects. Just beyond the pool, a forest of ponderosa pines stood tall and stately, calmly keeping watch.

"I don't see anything that looks like a rune gate," Darius said.

"It's beneath the water," I said. "And it will be there when I need it. I know it will."

"It's highly possible," Liam told Darius. "This realm is always shifting and rearranging. Gray's own magical realm could be in any location at any time. It's not fixed. Given that, her intuition and magic are our best—and really only —guides. If she says it will appear, I trust that it will."

"In that case..." Darius slipped his hand around the back of my neck and gave it a reassuring squeeze. "Lead the way, little brawler."

We headed down the hill in the direction of the pool, sticking close together, keeping watch in all directions. But everything about this place felt so calm, so peaceful. There were no monsters here. No ghosts. No traps.

Only the way home.

"Once we locate the rune gate," Liam said, "I'll go in first. We don't know how long it will take to travel through, and I want to be there when you arrive on the other side, just in case. Once we're together in your realm, we'll reconnect with the material plane like we've done in the past, and hopefully, return with your body *and* your soul."

"I'm coming with you," Darius said. "I don't like words like 'hopefully.'"

"I'm afraid you and Ronan can't access Gray's realm. You must return through the hell portal."

"I don't want to leave her," he said.

"I'm afraid you must. You can't go through her rune gate, and she can't go through the hell portal. To do so would—"

"Yes, I'm well aware of the risks." Darius let out a low growl of frustration. "Alright. Ronan will open the hell portal. Liam, you'll go through the rune gate. Then we'll send Gray through, and Ronan and I will follow through the portal."

"That's our best shot," I said. "And we'll all meet up on the other side. Right?"

Liam nodded. "Hopeful—"

"Shh!" I pressed my finger to his lips, laughing. "Don't say the H-word."

He grinned behind my fingers, then grabbed my hand, kissing my fingers. "As you wish."

Darius rolled his eyes. "You two *are* rather nauseating, aren't you? Are you going to carry on like this the entire way home?"

"Jealous, vampire?" I teased, elbowing him in the ribs.

"I am most certainly *not*. I'm merely stating—"

"He's here!" I shouted, spotting Ronan up ahead. He'd just exited the ponderosa forest and was heading toward the pool. I left Darius and Liam and broke into a run, my heart soaring, my magic swirling into a frenzy inside.

Ronan had seen me too, and now bolted toward me, the two of us on a collision course across the valley. I laughed, thinking of all the airport reunion scenes I'd seen in Sophie's rom-coms. All I needed was a cheesy soundtrack, and the moment would be complete.

We crashed into each other full force, toppling to the ground. Ronan wrapped me up in his arms, rolling me on top of him, holding me so tight I almost couldn't breathe. Tears streaked my cheeks, falling onto his face.

He took my face into his hands, staring up at me as if he couldn't believe I was real.

I knew the feeling.

"About time, demon," I teased, laughter breaking through my tears.

Without a word, he slid his fingers into my hair and pulled me to his mouth, devouring me with a kiss I felt all the way to my toes.

"You two are so disgustingly sweet you're giving me cavities," Darius teased as he and Liam finally caught up. "Really. All of you are just conspiring to make me ill on this trip."

"Don't listen to him," I told Ronan. "He's just jealous I didn't run into *his* arms when he got here."

"Jealous?" he repeated, his tone nearly indignant now. "You were barely conscious after having suffered dozens of broken bones and severe hypothermia. It was hardly the time for prancing across the meadow."

Still laughing, I got to my feet, Ronan by my side.

"Good to see you, Vacarro," Darius said, smacking Ronan on the back. All teasing aside, there was no true jealousy there. Only friendship. Only love.

Together, the four of us walked back to the Pool of Unknowing, the last rays of the sun slowly fading behind us, ushering in the cool evening.

"Why is it called the Pool of Unknowing?" I asked.

Liam glanced up at the sky, then back to me, lowering his voice. "It's the feeding ground for the memory eaters."

"That... sounds terrifying," I said.

"For those not traveling on to their final resting place, yes. But for most souls, it's a symbiotic relationship. The souls that travel through here must release the last of their earthly memories before completing their journey. Memory eater demons feed on those lingering memories."

"How do they feed?" I asked.

"They're absolutely *terrifying* creatures when they're hungry," Liam said. "Violent, vicious, incredibly dangerous. But the actual process of feeding is quite painless—pleasant, even. One must only look into their eyes, and his memories will be absorbed. The demons are then sated, and the souls are free to complete their journey, wholly unburdened."

"But I thought that's what the Orchard of Echoes was for," I said.

"Not exactly. The Orchard forces souls to confront their fears and regrets. Memory eaters take *all* lingering memories—the terrible ones as well as the beautiful."

"Why would someone want to give up their best memories?"

"Because they aren't real, Gray. They aren't needed. They are merely stories—"

"Um, guys?" Ronan said. "This is super fascinating. Truly. But we should probably..." He gestured toward the pool, and I nodded, blowing out a breath. Ronan was right —we needed to figure out how this was going to work. The faster we did that, the sooner we could all get home.

There would be plenty of time to ask about the memory eaters later, preferably from the comfort of a soft leather couch in front of a roaring fire, one of Emilio's warm, gooey brownies in my hand.

I opened my mouth to ask Liam what I should do, but

then realized I already knew the answer. The same gentle tug that had guided me through the realm called to me now, and I knelt before the stones surrounding the pool and peered inside. At first, I saw only the smooth, black surface of the water, completely undisturbed.

But soon it began to change colors, from black to deep indigo, with swirls of purple and lighter blue and turquoise, all of it sparkling with starlight just like I'd seen in my vision.

"Look!" I breathed.

Just below the surface, an archway of glowing runes appeared, pulsing bright. It looked as if someone had lain the archway on its back—as if we could dive right in and end up on the other side, safe in my own realm.

Home.

When I reached in and touched the water, my magic sparked to life, enveloping my hand in a bright blue orb. I pulled it back, and the water began to spin into a gentle whirlpool.

"Gray," Ronan said. "The water level's lowering."

"It's the magic," Liam said. "It's opening the gateway to her realm."

"Incredible," Darius whispered.

My heart sped up, my eyes wide, a sense of purpose and excitement and clarity rising from my chest, making my skin buzz.

But the moment the sun dipped fully behind the horizon, the grass at my knees turned pale with frost, and the pool froze, the stars winking out, the colors fading to solid white.

"No!" I leaned over the stones and pressed my hand to the surface again, but my magic flickered out, too.

The connection was broken.

A pang of sadness touched my heart, but it didn't last. I didn't need to see the gate to know it was there waiting for me. My magic had led us here for a reason. *This* was the way home. I knew it.

"The pool will thaw at sunrise," Liam confirmed. "We'll camp in the woods tonight, and head out at first light. *Immediately* at first light."

There was an ominous tone to his words that hadn't been there before.

"Liam?" I prodded.

"It's not wise to linger into the late morning," he said.

"Why? What's late morning?"

He glanced up at the sky again, and my entire body erupted in goosebumps. "Feeding time."

TWENTY-NINE

RONAN

"If we're camping, we need a fire." I glanced at Gray, hoping she'd get the hint. "I'm gonna go, ah, look for some firewood."

"I'll come with." She hopped up immediately, reaching out to take my hand.

That's my girl.

The forest was thick and silent, and after just a few minutes of walking, we had complete privacy.

"Firewood, huh?" she asked, her eyes glittering.

"Was I that obvious?"

"Only a *little* obvious."

I was still holding her hand, and now I tugged her close, wrapping my arms around her and crushing her against my chest. Even though we'd hugged in the valley, it still felt like it'd been a hundred years since I'd last felt the warmth of her body against mine.

"I was so worried about you," I whispered into her hair.

"When Liam told us you were Jonathan's prisoner, and then you ended up here…"

A shudder rolled through my body when I thought about what might've happened to her in that prison. What could've happened to her here, if she hadn't found the rune gate.

"Jonathan's dead," she said, pulling back to look into my eyes. Her own held a steadiness that hadn't been there before. A certainty. "I stabbed him on the mountaintop, right before Darius found me."

I blew out a breath, more relieved than I cared to admit. One lone hunter? We should've been able to isolate him and take him out on day one. Yet he'd eluded us, besting us at every turn. His capacity for torture and torment had shocked us all.

And we still didn't know who else might be following in his footsteps. What other horrors awaited us on the other side of all this.

But we'd cross that bridge when we came to it.

I took her face between my palms, my gaze sweeping down to her mouth. I wanted to burn this image into my brain, sear it so deep I'd never forget it, no matter what Sebastian did to me. No matter what our future held.

I lowered my mouth to hers, capturing it in a slow, lingering kiss. I wanted to savor every soft curve of her lips, the warmth of her breath, the velvet-smooth stroke of her tongue as I slid mine into her mouth.

A moan rumbled through my chest, and Gray sighed, deepening our kiss. I moved forward, backing her up against a tree, pressing my body to hers and pinning her there.

"I missed you," she breathed, tangling her hands into my hair. "I hate being away from you, Ronan."

My name was a soft sigh on her breath, the sound of it making me ache for her in more ways than one.

"I missed you, too."

She looked up at me through lowered lashes, her eyes darkening with desire. With raw, unfiltered lust.

Quirking her lips into a sexy grin, she slid her hand down my chest, dipping her fingers into the front of my pants. I was instantly hard, desperate to feel her, skin on skin.

"Gray," I moaned, kissing her again as her fingers closed around my cock. She tightened her grip, stroking me just right.

Her touch was perfect. *She* was perfect.

Fuck, I couldn't wait another minute. I had to be inside her. To feel the soft, wet heat of her body. To make her shudder around me. To feel her warmth, her energy, the spark of life that made her unmistakably Gray. Unmistakably *mine*.

Sebastian thought he could stop this. That he could wave his pen and his contracts and his threats in front of my face and dictate the boundaries of my own heart.

Hell, maybe he could. I'd made worse deals in my life. But this was the Shadowrealm, outside the bounds of all other laws—even his. There were no deals here, no bargains, no Prince of Hell lording over us.

Gray squeezed me tighter, a sigh of pleasure escaping her lips, and I couldn't hold back another second. I grabbed both of her hands and pinned her wrists up over her head, crushed her against the tree, rocking into her hips, claiming her hot, wet mouth in a kiss that made both of us weak.

"You good?" I panted, and when she replied, "God, yes. More than good," I pulled back just long enough to spin her around, facing her toward the tree. She put her hands against the bark and arched her back, and I hooked my fingers into the back of her cargo pants and tugged, sliding them down to reveal the soft, perfect mounds of her ass.

I nearly came at the sight of her bare flesh, her curves, the soft gasp she unleashed as the chilly air hit her skin.

She was fucking beautiful. Everything about her.

Gray deserved to be loved. She deserved to be worshipped and pleasured and touched, slowly and deliberately. She deserved to be laid on a bed of rose petals and made love to with a thousand kisses for a thousand nights.

I might never be able to give her that. But I could give her this, right here, right now, tucked away in the ponderosa forest in another realm where nothing else mattered but one raw, intense, wild moment.

I fumbled with my pants and freed my aching cock, sliding it between her thighs, teasing her entrance.

"Yes," she said, arching her backside higher to give me access. "Right there."

I didn't need to be told twice. I plunged inside, sinking deep into her slick, perfect heat. For one brief moment, I stilled, curling a hand around her hip, bracing the other against the tree, resting my head on her shoulder. This, too, I wanted to memorize. The sweet, butterscotch smell of the ponderosa pine mingling with her scent. The silky touch of her hair tickling my nose. The sound of her ragged breath cutting through the silence of the forest. The cool air on my skin. The perfect fit of her body, slowly tightening around me.

In the ancient span of my lifetime, I'd only known Gray for a few heartbeats. Yet somehow, the woman had become my entire world.

I grabbed both of her hips, then pulled back, slowly sliding inside her once again. Gray moaned in pleasure, but it wasn't enough. I needed more. Deeper. Harder.

I rolled my hips, increasing the intensity of my thrusts, slamming against her perfect ass. Gray braced herself against the tree and matched my fevered pace, pushing back into me, urging me to take more.

"Harder," she demanded.

I ran a hand up her back and fisted her hair, pulling her head backward as I slammed into her from behind, taking her hard and deep and *fuck* I never wanted to be more than a heartbeat away from this woman, this witch, this beautiful soul who'd claimed my heart so long ago I couldn't even remember a time when it hadn't beat just for her.

"Ronan!" she gasped. "That's... Yes! *Ronan!*"

I clamped a hand over her mouth, trying to quite her screams before the others came running. She teased my fingers with her tongue, then took them into her mouth, sucking me, stroking me, making me absolutely lose it.

"Fucking hell, woman. What are you doing to me?"

She bit down on my fingers as her body clenched tight around me, and I absolutely fucking lost it. I came hot and hard and fast, pumping into her as she trembled through her own orgasm, both of us sweating and wild and completely unbidden as if the entire realm had been created just for us. As if nothing else mattered but this brief moment of pure, uncut perfection.

When Gray finally turned around to face me again, she offered a smile that damn near melted my heart. Her cheeks were pink, her eyes dark and seductive, her skin glowing. Blonde curls stuck up in every direction, as if she'd just stepped out into a windstorm.

She looked like a damn wood sprite. Like something out of the pages of a fairy tale book about magical forests where monsters didn't exist, and the night was full of beauty and wonder instead of terror and pain.

I wanted to pin her down inside that book, to keep her just like this forever. Keep her safe. Keep her mine.

But I couldn't do that. So instead, I wrapped my arms around her and crushed her to my chest again, burying my face in her neck, inhaling her scent.

Fuck you, Sebastian. Fuck. You.

After spending lifetimes upon lifetimes as his demonic slave, I'd finally come to realize something about Sebastian's nature. He wasn't evil because he traded in souls and flesh. He was evil because he turned love into a weakness, a weapon he could use to twist and manipulate and bend others to his will. More than claiming my soul, more than lying to me for centuries about my origins, more than the abuse he doled out on every visit, *that* was the thing I most resented him for.

I'd fallen in love with Gray. And he'd taken her from me.

"I love you," I whispered, knowing full well this was the only place I could ever say it out loud again. I pressed my thumb against her lips and looked into her eyes and poured everything I felt into them, into her, wanting her to take these words and burn them deep inside her, like scars she'd carry long after we reached our inevitable end.

She stared into my eyes, her own shiny with tears. "I love you, too, Ronan. Always."

"Always." My heart cracked wide open at the word. It tasted like a lie. Not because I didn't mean it, but because *always* no longer belonged to us.

In truth, it never had.

THIRTY

GRAY

We're deep in the forest, tracking a white-tailed deer who's been eluding us for hours. Beneath the light of a full moon, my companion grins and holds a finger to his lips, and I peer out through the trees in the direction of his gaze.

The deer grazes in the clearing. A buck, with huge interlaced horns and a gleaming tawny coat.

He is beautiful in a way that makes my heart ache.

I step on a twig, snapping it, and the deer bolts.

"Hurry," my guide whispers, disappearing ahead, and I run to catch up. I don't want to disturb the buck, but I don't want to lose my way in this dark wood.

As long as the man is with me, I know I'm safe. He is my guide, and I trust him implicitly.

But I've lost him.

"Hello?" I call out. "Where are you?"

Something rustles the brush ahead, and I race toward the

sound. My guide is gone, and three women stand before me, all dressed in white, each holding a silver sword.

The first one is blonde like me, with long, muscular legs and expressive brown eyes.

The second has the same expressive eyes, but her hair is dark, wrapped in a braid around the top of her head.

The last is thin and pale, her dark head shorn. While the others are wearing dresses, she's dressed in a hospital gown. There's something so familiar about her, but I just can't place it.

"Don't follow him," they say in unison. "He is not what you believe."

I look down in my hands. I'm holding a sword too, but I don't want it. I don't need it. I toss it at their feet and run to catch up with my guide.

He's waiting for me at the edge of the clearing, but as soon as I get close, he smiles at me and disappears into the trees again.

He's teasing me.

I don't mind.

I mean to follow him into the trees, but the women are before me again, blocking my way.

"Don't follow," they say, their swords piercing the earth at their feet. Again, a sword appears in my hand.

Again, I drop it.

"Let me be," I hiss. I dart around them, continuing on the path toward the trees where my guide disappeared.

"This way," his voice calls out, light and teasing. He's enjoying this game.

"Where are you?" I call out, peeking behind a massive oak tree.

"This way!" he calls again from farther ahead. *"Over here!"*

I run to catch up, scrambling up a steep trail. When I reach the top of the rise, he's there waiting for me, and I'm rewarded with a smile

"Where is the deer?" I ask.

His smile turns cold.

"I'm sorry," he says. "It was you. It was always you."

"What?" I reach out for him, but before I can take another step closer, a shadow in the shape of a man leaps out from the trees behind him. He's carrying three swords, and with a single thrust, he lunges for me, driving the blades through my chest.

I drop to my knees, gasping.

It happens so fast, I don't feel the pain. Just the shock, followed by the rush of air leaving my lungs, and the warmth of my blood as it runs down my legs and seeps into the earth.

Roses bloom in its path, growing large and fragrant, tangling in my fingers, my hair, swallowing me back into the earth.

Overhead, the full moon smiles.

I awoke with a startled gasp, my heart hammering in my chest, my hands pressed to what I was certain would be a gaping wound.

"Gray!" Ronan sat up next to me on our bed of leaves, taking my face into his hands. "What is it?"

"Just… a nightmare," I breathed. But God, it had been so real. The forest, the swords, the shadow. The three women. The three swords.

Wait, no... There had been four swords at first. I'd had one, too.

Four swords... Four of swords...

Sophie's tarot reading echoed through my memory.

There are four of you, she'd said. *The swords represent four witches. Three standing their ground, waiting for the fourth to rise, to find them and give them purpose...*

I closed my eyes, thinking back on that tarot reading. Sophie was so certain I was one of the four, that I needed to find the others. But who were they? How could I find them? What was I supposed to do?

The three of swords had turned up in that same tarot reading. Was that the shadow man? Some terrible betrayal I'd yet to endure? To even suspect?

I shivered at the thought, my whole body going cold.

"It's okay," Ronan said softly, rubbing slow circles on my back. "We're going home soon. Just breathe."

I relaxed back onto the leaves, letting him wrap his arms around me and nuzzle my neck. His body was warm and firm, his touch protective. We'd spent the night here with the others, all of us huddled together for warmth, but now there was just the two of us.

"Where are Liam and Darius?" I asked.

"Just checking things out at the pool. Sun's almost up."

I nodded. Today was the day we'd all go home.

So why did my heart feel so heavy?

Ronan kissed my neck. "Better?"

"A little," I whispered, allowing myself a few minutes to

sink into the pleasure of this moment, his arms around me, his breath stirring my hair.

The pre-dawn sky was a pale shade of pink, the last of the stars winking out. All around us, white puffs of steam rose from the forest floor, the frost already beginning to melt.

It wouldn't be long until the sun was up. The pool would thaw, my gate would appear, and we would be on our way.

"Do you think Asher's okay?" I asked.

Ronan was silent a few beats. Then he pressed a kiss to my shoulder and said, "I think if he wasn't, we would know it. We'd feel it."

I nodded, but I wasn't completely convinced.

"I've seen Ash fight his way out of more fucked-up situations than a hunter prison," he said. "And now he's got something even more important to fight for. *Someone.*"

This got a smile, and Ronan leaned in close, lowering his mouth to mine and feathering a gentle kiss across my lips.

We got up gingerly, picking leaves out of each other's hair and slowly warming up to the morning.

"We good?" He pulled me into a hug and flashed a grin, but it wasn't as good as his old ones, and it wasn't enough to chase off the lingering cobwebs of my nightmare. I couldn't stop thinking about the shadow man, the swords, the ending.

I smiled at him anyway, tucking my head into the spot where his shoulder met his neck and telling myself it was just a bad dream. That this entire nightmare of Shadowrealm banishment, hunter prisons, and witch murders would soon be over.

That we could actually make a life together where our toughest challenge wasn't fighting off hunters or rescuing prisoners or breaking demon contracts, but simply finding a bed big enough to fit us all.

It was a crazy dream, and I probably should've known better than to let it sneak past my heart's defenses.

But I could already feel it taking root. Blooming. A fragile, green bud shooting up from the darkness, seeking the light.

THIRTY-ONE

LIAM

The sun had risen, the ice had begun to melt, and the bright blue runes on Gray's gateway flickered faintly beneath the surface of the pool, just as Gray had predicted.

"It's almost time," I told her. Ronan and Darius were just inside the woods, seeking the best place to open the hell portal. Once the ice fully melted and the gateway was accessible, we'd set our plan into motion. "Are you ready?"

"I'm not sure." Gray's eyes were full of concerns, haunted by shadows. "I can't shake the feeling that something's just... off."

"It's natural to have doubts, Gray. Nothing like this has ever been attempted before."

"Do you think we're crazy to even try?"

I considered her question. Thought about all the reasons why I might've said yes. Why I *should've* said yes.

"There was a time I might have thought so," I admitted.

"And now?"

"You've made it this far. You've beaten the odds at every turn. I think you'd be crazy *not* to try."

Gray's smile felt like my own personal sunrise, a beautiful dawn I wasn't sure I deserved to look upon. "Thank you, Liam. For everything you've done for me. I don't know where I'd be without your guidance. Your friendship."

She took my hand, squeezing gently. That odd sensation in my chest took hold again, making my heart race. *My* heart. I could no longer call it Liam's. After all this time in his body, I wasn't sure I could separate the two.

I wasn't sure I wanted to.

I slipped away from her touch. Like her smile, I wasn't sure I deserved it. "Everything I thought I knew about you, about your destiny... I was wrong, Gray. I'm afraid I've misled you at every turn."

"No, Liam. You haven't. You couldn't have known how things would turn out. None of us knew." She laughed. "I mean, did you ever think I'd be here in the Shadowrealm, fully manifested? And that I'd find a way back to my own realm? Did you ever think I'd be free of Jonathan? That Ronan and Darius would be here with us right now?"

"No, I suppose not."

Her eyes turned mischievous, and she lowered her voice. "Did you ever think we'd kiss?"

"No," I whispered. I felt myself blushing, desperately wishing I could tell her how badly I wanted to kiss her again. How badly I wanted to take her in my arms like I'd seen the others do so many times, like it was the most

268

natural thing in the world. How badly I needed to know that it meant as much to her as it had to me. That there might come a time where I would look upon her face and see the same look in her eyes that I'd seen that day on the beach.

But I knew that time would never come. Not for us.

"There's something you need to know," I said. The time had come. I could put it off no longer. "I'd always meant to tell you. I just... I truly thought we'd have more time."

"What is it, Liam? You know you can tell me anything."

I smiled softly, wrapping a lock of her hair around my finger. It was such a simple gesture, but it reminded me what it was like to be alive. Truly alive.

"Your hair is like a sunrise," I said. "Like pure golden light."

"Okay, now you're scaring me." She laughed, but the sound of it was tight and nervous, nothing like the beautiful music I'd grown to love.

Tell her, you fool. Tell her before it's too late.

"Gray, I need you to understand something about me. I'm not—"

"Liam. Gray." Darius emerged from the woods. "Ronan is ready to open the hell portal."

I nodded once, then turned back to Gray. The last of the pool's ice had melted, and now the runes glowed brightly.

It was time.

"To be continued?" She stretched up on her toes, pressing a soft kiss to the corner of my lips. "When we get back?"

When we get back. She'd said it as if there was a place where we'd always belonged together, where I'd always been part of her life. A place where we'd be free to get to know each other. Maybe even fall in love.

I didn't have the heart to tell her that it didn't exist. Not for us.

"I... Of course. To be continued." I squeezed her hand and returned her gentle, trusting smile, hoping against the odds that I'd have the opportunity to explain everything before it was too late.

Hoping I'd have the opportunity to confess.

To apologize.

And to beg her forgiveness, in this realm or the next.

THIRTY-TWO

EMILIO

"This isn't just some black market fae magic Jonathan picked up on the streets," I said to Elena. "Darkwinter are working with the hunters to hybridize supernaturals and create large-scale magical weapons. They're planning an all-out war."

My sister set two mugs of coffee on the dining room table, taking the seat across from me. It was well after midnight. I'd just returned from my disastrous meeting with Talia, and she'd just returned from her office, but neither of us would be getting sleep anytime soon.

"The situation is serious," Elena said. "Finding the witches and the other hostages is paramount. Solving the murders is paramount. As is keeping an eye on the hunters and fae in the Cape." She sipped her coffee, then met my eyes across the table. "But let's try to keep things in perspective, Emilio."

"What perspective?"

"One devil's trap is hardly a large-scale magical weapon."

"No. It's a prototype. As are his experiments. He's torturing witches and supernaturals in order to create some kind of... *super* supernaturals."

"I'm not following." She set down her mug, her finger-nails clicking on the sides. "Is he trying to kill supers, or make them more powerful?"

"I think he's doing both."

"To what end, Emilio?"

"What else? Power. Control." I rose from the table, pacing once again. "Talia can no longer be trusted. I'm not sure any of them can. I'm telling you, Elena. This goes all the way up to the top."

"To the Council?"

I nodded, but the pit in my stomach told me it went even beyond that.

"You're talking about a conspiracy," she said.

"That's exactly what I'm talking about. Think about it, Elena. If you wanted to weaken the supernatural communities, what's the fastest way to go?"

"Humans," she said without hesitation. "Reveal our existence, paint us as the enemy that wants to eat their children and destroy their way of life, then arm them." She shrugged, casually sipping her coffee as if we really *were* dealing in hypotheticals. "Nothing excites and unifies angry, repressed humans with too much time on their hands like finding a common enemy."

"Under normal circumstances, yes. But I asked about

the *fastest* way." I sat down again, pulling my chair closer to her. "Think about how long it would take to use humans. We're talking about a mass scale here, not just some neighborhood punks taking out a few vampires or smashing up a fae club. Before they could roll out a widespread hate campaign against us, first they'd have to convince humans that we even exist at all. We're talking months. Years."

Elena opened her mouth to argue—her default response with me—but then closed it, nodding. I could practically hear the pieces clicking into place in her mind.

"Destroy us from the inside out," she said suddenly. "That's the fastest way. Turn all of us against each other, then sit back and watch us do the heavy lifting. Let us kill each other."

"Bingo."

"So how does a ragtag bunch of hunters and dark fae pull this off? Even with the Council looking the other way, they just don't have the numbers for such a coordinated effort."

"The witches are key," I said, "because taking them out gives these guys several advantages. First of all, it immediately upsets the power balance. Witches are guardians of magic, so their mere presence in a community helps keep things in balance. Remove them from the equation, and things start to go downhill real fast.

"We're already experiencing it in Blackmoon Bay. Soon after the murders, we got hit with a supernatural crime wave." I told her about the vampire attacks, the vandalism, the arson, all the shit we were still trying to get a handle on back home.

"And that's just in the Bay," I continued. "Picture the same thing happening in cities across the country. Across the world, even." I remembered what Gray had said about what she'd read in Sophie's book of shadows. "Some of the Bay Coven witches have thought for a long time that the hunters were joining forces again, possibly planning a more coordinated attack."

After doubting me for so long, minimizing this entire situation, Elena looked positively stricken.

"Now you've got utter global chaos," I continued. "Everything is completely destabilized. The few humans who *did* know about us—those who lived and worked alongside us—are now fearing for their lives, and with good reason. From there, it wouldn't take much to get the rest of the humans on board with the fear campaign, but that would just be the icing on the cake. The real damage would've been done already. Done by our own people."

"You're right," she said. "God, Emilio. You're right. When everything is completely destabilized and the humans are hiding in fear from the big bad monsters, the Council and their chosen few will sweep in and offer a so-called better way. Stability. Safety. They'll re-establish the rule of law according to their own needs."

"Not just the Council and the chosen few," I said. "But the hybrids they themselves created through their partner-ship with the hunters. They'll have an army, Elena. They're using the witches' magic to create these uber-powerful supernaturals that have the best and strongest powers from each of us. Vampires that can shift into wolves, impervious to both hawthorn and silver? Shifters that can cast spells and travel to alternate dimensions? Demons that can resurrect themselves?"

My sister gaped at me, fear flickering in her otherwise steely gaze. "Emilio, if Talia's involved in all this, and you just made yourself her enemy—"

The buzz of the doorbell startled us both.

My sister took a deep breath, scenting the air.

"One of yours?" I asked.

"There's no signature."

We got up together, both unholstering our guns at the same time, slowly creeping toward the door.

"There's no need for weapons," a male voice said, so clear and refined it could only be fae. "I come as a friend from Blackmoon Bay."

With Elena backing me up, I cracked open the door to find a figure standing on the porch in a black cape, his hands held up in surrender.

"I'm here on behalf of the few remaining fae who don't wish to start an all-out war," the visitor said. He lowered the hood on his cape, revealing his stark white hair and yellow eyes.

"Jael?" I hadn't seen the Seelie prince since I'd interviewed him at Illuminae right after Sophie's murder, and seeing him here in Raven's Cape, standing on my sister's front porch like some kind of Halloween trick-or-treater... It was so out of context I didn't know what the hell to do next.

I was literally frozen, staring at him with my mouth open, my hand still tightly gripping my gun.

"It wasn't supposed to be like this, Detective Alvarez," he said. "Not for any of us."

I scrutinized his face, noting the concern in his eyes. He was telling the truth.

I stepped back, inviting him inside and quickly introducing my sister.

"What brings you all the way out here?" Elena asked.

"As much as I hate human colloquialisms," Jael said, "I'm afraid your brother has just kicked the hornet's nest."

THIRTY-THREE

GRAY

Using Sophie's dagger, Ronan sliced open his palm, squeezing blood onto the ground at the edge of the forest not far from the pool. The soft whisper of his demonic incantations floated on the breeze, making the blood glow a bright, blazing orange.

He knelt down and pressed his palm flat against the ground.

Light blasted outward from his touch, and the portal flickered into view in front of us, a great swirling hole that glowed the same blazing shade as his blood.

"There she is. The way home." Ronan got to his feet and cleaned the dagger, then handed it back to me.

Sliding it back into the sheath I'd strapped to my thigh, I said, "So that's it? You guys just… step into the light?"

I peered inside, mesmerized. There was no beginning, no end. Only light. Infinite, blazing light.

"Precisely." Darius put a firm hand on my shoulder. "But I'd feel much better if you took a few steps back, love."

I did as he asked, rubbing a sudden chill from my arms. I didn't want to get sucked into the hell portal—not when I was so close to getting back to my own realm.

"Gray, the gate is ready," Liam called.

We joined him at the pool, the portal in full view. Beneath the water, my rune gate pulsed lightly, stirring the magic inside me. It felt like a ball of energy in my chest, and I took a deep breath, willing it to expand. To fill me.

The same blue orbs burst to life on my palms, and I laughed, feeling lighter and hopeful. We were really doing this.

The water swirled with color and starlight, just like it had yesterday. I dipped my glowing hands in briefly, then pulled back, watching the water spin into its lazy whirlpool. Moments later, it began to drain, revealing the stone archway that would lead us into my realm.

"Are you sure you want to go first?" I asked Liam.

"I must," he said. "But I promise I'll be waiting for you on the other side. Once we reunite there, we'll need to shut it so nothing follows you through."

I nodded, remembering his warning about the memory eaters and feeding time. I did *not* want one of those beasts slipping into my magic place.

"Then I guess this is goodbye," I said. "For now."

I pulled Liam into a quick hug, but he held on a beat longer. When we finally broke apart, he looked into my eyes for one last moment, as if he were trying to memorize my face. He opened his mouth and took a breath, but then closed it.

The water had completely drained. The magic faded from my hands.

Without another word, Liam turned and climbed onto the stones surrounded the pool.

Then he jumped, vanishing into the depths.

"You're next, vampire," Ronan said.

"Gray should go next," Darius said. "I want to be sure she gets through."

"There's no time for that. She can't go through until we're sure Liam's through. As long as he doesn't return, she's good to go. In the meantime, you're next."

Reluctantly, Darius agreed.

We headed back to the hell portal, still blazing at the edge of the forest.

"Safe travels," Ronan said, offering Darius a brief nod before stepping aside to give Darius and me some privacy.

I appreciated that more than he knew.

I took his hands in mine, looking up into his golden eyes.

"When you get back," I said, "Tell Emilio—"

He cut off my words with a fierce, possessive kiss that left me breathless. When he finally broke away, he said, "You tell him yourself when you get back. We'll have a big celebration, complete with brownies *and* wine. And then I'm taking you to New York, just like we said. So you'd better get back home safe, Miss Desario, or you're really going to screw up my plans."

He touched his forehead to mine, stroking my cheek with his knuckles. Tears blurred my vision.

"To think I used to be afraid of you," I said, smiling at the memory.

"So you've told me. Multiple times." Darius grinned. "And now?"

I pulled back and met his eyes again, my heart thumping. For so long, I was convinced that loving someone meant giving up some precious part of yourself, something you'd never be able to get back.

I'd wasted so much time being afraid of it, even as it was wrapping me in its embrace. I'd been scared to tell Ronan how I felt about him. Scared to let myself fall for anyone else. Scared that loving more than one man at the same time meant I was confused or fooling myself or just plain weird.

But all those fears were for nothing.

Love made you stronger. It made you believe in things that shouldn't have been possible. And even here, in the most desperate, hopeless place, it made you feel alive in a way that nothing else could.

"I love you, Darius," I said. The words came out in a rush, leaving me as hot and breathless as his kiss, filling me with warmth.

I was no longer afraid of those three little words. Saying them had set me free, and as soon as we were all back on the same plane again, I was going to say them again, to each and every one of my rebels. To Haley and Reva. To all of the people who'd let me into their hearts, even when I was doing my best to lock them out of mine.

"Gray," he whispered, the soft caress of his breath warm and perfect against my lips. "It seems I've fallen in—"

"Gray! Move!" Ronan's panicked shout shattered the moment, and before I could take my next breath, Darius had me on the ground, shielding me with his body as the creature trampled over us, bolting right past.

It was the size and shape of a wolf, with patchy, matted fur and a partial skull that caved in on one side. Its stride was strong and powerful, but uneven. It left a trail of blood behind.

Dread pooled in my gut.

It couldn't be him...

From the corner of my eye, I saw Ronan lunge for it, but the thing evaded him easily.

"Why isn't it attacking?" Darius asked, pulling me to my feet and stepping in front of me protectively. "What the hell is it?"

"Shit! It's heading for the pool," Ronan said, sprinting after it.

"Ronan, wait!" I charged after him, Darius by my side.

The beast wasn't just heading for the pool. He was heading for my rune gate.

"It's Jonathan," I breathed, all of the wind rushing out of my lungs. "Get him, Ronan! Don't let him through!"

Ronan launched himself at Jonathan's twisted form, Darius bolting after them with superhuman speed. They hit the beast at the same time, bringing him down.

I ran to catch up.

"Stay back, Gray."

"It's Jonathan," I said again. "He's turned himself into a shifter."

"And a vampire," Darius said, struggling to keep his hold. "He's got vamp fangs."

"I thought I killed him," I said, still in shock.

"If he's got vamp in him," Darius said, "we have to burn him or behead him."

Snapping out of my stupor, I went for the dagger at my thigh, but Jonathan refused to be pinned down. He shot out of their grasp, snarling and snapping, dodging at every turn.

"I can't fucking catch him!" Ronan shouted. "Grab him, Beaumont!"

Darius was no more than a blur in my peripheral vision, but so was Jonathan.

The last thing I saw was his twisted, mutilated body launching over the stones, disappearing into the pool below.

I charged after him, ready to jump in and fight. Ready to chase him down in my own realm and take his head, once and for all.

But before I could even talk myself out of that idea, a great darkness blotted out the sun, and Ronan was shouting at me once again.

"Down! Get down!"

I dropped to the ground and covered my head just as a huge, winged beast swooped past me, clipping my shoulder with its monstrous hoof.

Ignoring the shock of pain, I unsheathed the dagger and rolled onto my back, holding the knife close to my chest.

The beast was airborne again, circling, joined now by two others.

"Memory eaters," I gasped.

The creatures were awesome in the truest sense of the word—winged horses with sleek midnight-black bodies and silver manes and tails, and great gossamer wings that glittered in the sun. I watched them circle overhead, then dive, but I was no longer afraid.

I wanted to see them up close. To look into their eyes and seek out the depths of their magnificent beauty. To let them take away the last of my earthly burdens.

The blade trembled in my hands.

"Gray! Move!" Darius ran past me, scooping me up and shoving me out of the way just as one of the great beasts landed on the ground beside us. It sighed and whinnied, then shook its massive head, silver mane catching the light. A thousand galaxies glittered in its eyes.

I dropped my blade. Fell to my knees.

"Don't look into its eyes!" Darius shouted, but it was too late. The creature was so beautiful. So peaceful. Why would I look anywhere else?

Slowly, I felt something tingling in my mind, like warm water seeping into my skull.

Don't carry these burdens, sweet girl…

The warmth vanished in a blink, and I looked up to see Darius tearing out the beast's throat. Blood gushed from the wound, and a moment later, the memory eater collapsed to the ground.

Behind him, Ronan had leaped onto the back of the second beast. In a burst of raw demon strength, he grabbed the beast's head and twisted, snapping its neck. The thing crashed to the ground with so much force, the earth trembled.

"Gray!" Darius was at my side, shaking me out of the momentary trance. He picked up my blade and handed it to me. "Are you hurt?"

I looked into his eyes and shook my head, trying not to look at the blood covering his mouth and chest.

"What's my name?" he asked.

"Are you serious?"

"I need you to say it."

"My memories are intact, *Darius*," I said.

"Good. Now take cover and stay out of sight." He was gone in a blink, charging after the third beast. The moment the creature's hooves touched the ground, Darius was on him again, tearing out his throat.

Another shadow darkened the sun, and when I looked up into the sky, I saw half-a-dozen more memory eaters circling.

"Guys!" I shouted. "We've got a problem!"

The three of us regrouped in the valley, keeping our backs together, our eyes on the sky.

"We can't take them all at once," Darius said. "Not by force."

"What about influence?" Ronan asked him. "Maybe you can convince them to move on."

"I've tried. They're too big. I doubt they even felt my presence. If I could amplify—"

"Guys! You're brilliant." The idea came to me in a rush, half-formed and completely crazy, but worth a shot. I handed Darius Sophie's dagger. "I need your blood. Please don't ask questions."

He held my gaze for a second, but then nodded, slicing his wrist and pressing it to my mouth.

I began to suck, feeling the warm liquid fill my mouth, then sink into me as it had in the cabin. Magic stirred to life inside me.

I pulled away from him, closing my eyes and calling the magic forth, trusting our fate to the blood bond Darius and I shared. Trusting that I could channel his power. That I could amplify it.

This would work. It *had* to work.

I raised my hands, blue orbs igniting, then turning into flames that blasted out into the sky just as the creatures descended. I hit them with the full brunt of the magic, lighting them up in a fiery, bright blue beam that trapped them mid-air, suspending them above us.

> *My blood is his and his is mine*
> *Grant me his power, just for a time*
> *Lend me his strength, his control over minds*
> *Channeled through me, these creatures we'll bind*

I said the words, then reached out for their minds, searching for a way in.

You don't want this, I thought. *You've already fed. It's time to move on.*

The winged horses hovered before me, flapping their great wings.

I felt them resisting, trying to slip into my mind again. Warm, gentle, tendrils crept inside, curling around my memories, tugging gently.

You don't need this, sweet girl. Let us unburden you…

I hesitated, and two of the creatures broke free from my fiery hold, torpedoing toward us.

Ronan and Darius met them head on, wrestling them to the ground, attacking with vicious fury.

Again, I felt them slipping into my mind, prying.

Just relax. Let go. We shall ease your passage…

"No!" I shouted, slamming a mental wall into place and focusing the very last of my energy on one final pulse of magic.

Leave us, I thought, sending it up through my hands, out into the sky. Into them. *You are not needed here. You are needed elsewhere. You must go. You must leave us.*

I repeated the thoughts, again and again and again, my energy rapidly draining.

I collapsed to my knees with weakness, but still, I didn't give up, didn't relent.

Finally, I felt the last of their resistance break. The four remaining beasts flapped their wings, reared back in the sky, and flew away.

The magic dissipated, leaving me spent and exhausted. I wanted nothing more than to curl up in the grass and sleep for a thousand years.

But I needed to find the guys. To get home.

I got to my feet and jogged back toward the pool, where two hulking black forms lay dead in a cloud of dust. Ronan and Darius stood behind them, trying to catch their breath.

I sat on the stone perimeter encircling the pool and closed my eyes, waiting for my own breath to return, for my heartbeat to slow.

When the dust settled and I could finally breathe again, I got to my feet and turned toward the pool, peering inside.

At nothing.

No water. No starlight. No rune gate. The majestic Pool of Unknowing was no more than a pit filled with dust and emptiness.

The gateway—my last chance, my only road home—was gone.

I looked to Darius, the shock washing over me in waves.

"It's gone," I said, my voice breaking.

Darius blinked.

"The rune gate," I explained. "The pool. The way home."

He said nothing, still blinking at me in confusion.

I stepped closer, peering up into his eyes. "Darius?"

His brow furrowed as he looked around, taking in the scene. When he met my eyes again, his gaze was completely blank.

Moments ago at the hell portal, he'd looked at me like I

was the only thing that ever mattered. He'd almost said he was falling in love with me.

Now he looked at me like he'd never seen me before in his life.

"Pardon me," he said, stiff and formal. "But I seem to have lost my way. Would you mind telling me where I am?"

"Darius?" I said again, my mind refusing to believe it, even as my heart slowly cracked in two.

"Darius?" He looked over his shoulder, then back to me, shaking his head in confusion. He opened his mouth, then closed it, his lips twisting in disgust. "Is this... is this blood?"

Both pieces of my broken heart slammed against my ribs, the full realization punching a hole right through my chest.

Darius could speak, but he had no memories. He didn't know me. Didn't know his name. Didn't even know he was a vampire.

"Oh, fuck," Ronan said as he approached the pool, shaking the dust from his clothes. "The rune gate—"

"Ronan." I grabbed his arm, tugging him away from the pool. "Darius is... He's... The memory eaters..." A sob escaped my mouth, cutting off my words.

Ronan reached for me, his face crumpling in confusion and concern, but before I could get the rest of the words out, a terrible shriek pierced the air, driving us both to our knees.

The sky turned black, and I could tell from the sheer horror on Ronan's face what that meant.

The memory eaters had returned.

With a herd.

We shot to our feet.

"Get Darius!" I shouted. "He doesn't understand!"

Ronan grabbed Darius's hand. "Let's go. Run! Now!"

The three of us bolted for the forest, stopping just before the hell gate. I turned to look over my shoulder. The herd was bearing down on us, ten beasts across and at least that many deep. They were going to destroy us.

"Gray," Ronan whispered, and I turned back toward him, his hazel eyes glassy with emotion. For a moment, time seemed to stop, and the entire realm fell silent and still. "I'm so sorry."

I offered him a faint smile, my own tears falling freely. For Ronan. For Darius. For all of us.

"I know," I whispered.

Time started up again. The memory eaters howled their terrifying war cry, the force of their wings blowing back my hair, rustling the trees beyond.

With one hand clamped on Darius's arm, Ronan grabbed me around the waist, hauling me against his chest.

"Don't let go!" he shouted.

And then we jumped into the blazing light.

Straight into hell.

How will the rebels survive the trip through the hell portal, and who will be left standing on the other side? The story continues in *Blood Cursed*, book four of the Witch's Rebels series. **Get Blood Cursed Now!**

* * *

If you loved reading this story as much as I loved writing it, please help a girl out and **leave a review on Amazon!** Even a quick sentence or two about your favorite part can help other readers discover the book, and that makes me super happy!

XOXO
Sarah

ORIGINS OF THE WITCH'S REBELS

I was primarily inspired to write this series by three things: my fascination with Tarot, my love of all things witchy, and my desire to see more kickass women telling stories for and about other kickass women.

I've always enjoyed books, movies, and TV shows about witches, monsters, and magic, but I never found exactly the right mix. I wanted a darker, grittier Charmed, an older Buffy, and most of all—as much as I love the brothers Winchester (who doesn't?)—I *really* wanted a Supernatural with badass bitches at the helm, hunting monsters, battling their inner demons, and of course, sexytimes. Lots and lots of sexytimes.

(Side note: there's not enough romance on Supernatural. Why is that? Give me five minutes in that writers' studio…)

Anyway, back to The Witch's Rebels. We were talking about badass bitches getting the sexytimes they deserve.

Right.

So I started plotting my own story and fleshing out the character who would eventually become our girl Gray, thinking I had it all figured out. But as I dove deeper into the writing, and I really got to know Gray, Darius, Ronan, Asher, Emilio, and Liam, I discovered a problem. A big one.

With so many strong, sexy guys in the mix, I couldn't decide which one would be the hero to win Gray's heart. I loved them all as much as she did!

I agonized over this.

It felt like the worst kind of love triangle. Er, love rhombus? Love—wait. What's the word for five of them? Pentagon! Yes, a love pentagon.

Pure torture!

But then I had my lightbulb moment. In the face of so much tragedy and danger, Gray fights hard to open herself up to love, to trust people, to earn those hard-won friendships. Her capacity for giving and receiving love expands infinitely throughout the story, so why the hell *shouldn't* she be able to share that with more than one man?

There was no reason to force her to choose.

So, she doesn't. And her story will continue!

You, dear reader, don't have to choose either—that's part of the fun of reverse harem stories like this. But if you happen to have a soft spot for a particular guy, I'd love to hear about it!

Drop me a line anytime at sarah@sarahpiperbooks.com and tell me who's winning your heart so far! I'll tell you mine if you tell me yours! *wink wink*

Paranormal romance fans, I've got even more sexy books ready to heat up your bookshelf!

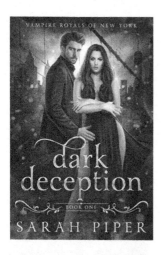

VAMPIRE ROYALS OF NEW YORK is a scorching paranormal romance series featuring a commanding, dirty-talking vampire king and the seductive thief who might just bring him to ruin… or become his eternal salvation. Sizzling romance, dark secrets, and hot vampires with British accents abound!

TAROT ACADEMY is a paranormal, university-aged reverse harem academy romance starring four seriously hot mages and one badass witch. Dark prophecies, unique mythology, steamy romance, strong female friendships, and plenty of supernatural thrills make this series a must-read!

ABOUT SARAH PIPER

Sarah Piper is a Kindle All-Star winning urban fantasy and paranormal romance author. Through her signature brew of dark magic, heart-pounding suspense, and steamy romance, Sarah promises a sexy, supernatural escape into a world where the magic is real, the monsters are sinfully hot, and the witches always get their magically-ever-afters.

Her works include the newly released Vampire Royals of New York series, the Tarot Academy series, and The Witch's Rebels, a fan-favorite reverse harem urban fantasy series readers have dubbed "super sexy," "imaginative and original," "off-the-walls good," and "delightfully wicked in the best ways," a quote Sarah hopes will appear on her tombstone.

Originally from New York, Sarah now makes her home in northern Colorado with her husband (though that changes frequently) (the location, not the husband), where she spends her days sleeping like a vampire and her nights writing books, casting spells, gazing at the moon, playing with her ever-expanding collection of Tarot cards, binge-watching Supernatural (Team Dean!), and obsessing over the best way to brew a cup of tea.

You can find her online at SarahPiperBooks.com and in her Facebook readers group, Sarah Piper's Sassy Witches! If you're sassy, or if you need a little *more* sass in your life, or if you need more Dean Winchester gifs in your life (who doesn't?), come hang out!

Made in the USA
Monee, IL
21 April 2021